**Jacob Grimm**

**Grimm's Fairy Stories**

**Jacob Grimm**

**Grimm's Fairy Stories**

# GRIMM'S FAIRY STORIES

## BY

## JACOB GRIMM

# Contents

| | | |
|---|---|---|
| Chapter I. | The Goose-Girl | 1 |
| Chapter II | The Little Brother And Sister | 7 |
| Chapter III | Hansel And Grethel | 12 |
| Chapter IV | Oh, If I Could But Shiver! | 18 |
| Chapter V | Dummling And The Three Feathers | 26 |
| Chapter VI | Little Snow White | 31 |
| Chapter VII | Catherine And Frederick | 37 |
| Chapter VIII | The Valiant Little Tailor | 44 |
| Chapter IX | Little Red Cap | 52 |
| Chapter X | The Golden Goose | 55 |
| Chapter XI | Bearskin | 58 |
| Chapter XII | Cinderella | 63 |
| Chapter XIII | Faithful John | 68 |
| Chapter XIV | The Water Of Life | 74 |
| Chapter XV | Thumbling | 79 |
| Chapter XVI | Briar Rose | 83 |
| Chapter XVII | The Six Swans | 86 |
| Chapter XVIII | Rapunzel | 91 |
| Chapter XIX | Mother Holle | 95 |
| Chapter XX | The Frog Prince | 98 |
| Chapter XXI | The Travels Of Tom Thumb | 102 |
| Chapter XXII | Snow-White And Rose-Red | 108 |
| Chapter XXIII | The Three Little Men In The Wood | 115 |

Chapter XXIV    Rumpelstiltskin                                      121

Chapter XXV     Little One-Eye, Two-Eyes And Three-Eyes             125

# GRIMM'S FAIRY STORIES

## By

## JACOB GRIMM

## THE GOOSE-GIRL

An old queen, whose husband had been dead some years, had a beautiful daughter. When she grew up, she was betrothed to a prince who lived a great way off; and as the time drew near for her to be married, she got ready to set off on her journey to his country. Then the queen, her mother, packed up a great many costly things—jewels, and gold, and silver, trinkets, fine dresses, and in short, everything that became a royal bride; for she loved her child very dearly; and she gave her a waiting-maid to ride with her, and give her into the bridegroom's hands; and each had a horse for the journey. Now the princess' horse was called Falada, and could speak.

When the time came for them to set out, the old queen went into her bed-chamber, and took a little knife, and cut off a lock of her hair, and gave it to her daughter, saying, "Take care of it, dear child; for it is a charm that may be of use to you on the road." Then they took a sorrowful leave of each other, and the princess put the lock of her mother's hair into her bosom, got upon her horse, and set off on her journey to her bridegroom's kingdom.

One day, as they were riding along by the side of a brook, the princess began to feel very thirsty, and said to her maid, "Pray get down and fetch me some water in my golden cup out of yonder brook, for I want to drink." "Nay," said the maid, "if you are thirsty, get down yourself, and lie down by the water and drink; I shall not be your waiting-maid any longer." The princess was so thirsty that she got down, and knelt over the little brook and drank, for she was frightened, and dared not bring out her golden cup; and then she wept, and said, "Alas! what will become of me?" And the lock of hair answered her, and said—

> "Alas! alas! if thy mother knew it,
> Sadly, sadly her heart would rue it."

But the princess was very humble and meek, so she said nothing to her maid's ill behavior, but got upon her horse again.

Then all rode further on their journey, till the day grew so warm, and the sun so scorching, that the bride began to feel very thirsty again; and at last, when they came to a river, she forgot her maid's rude speech, and said, "Pray get down and fetch me some water to drink in my golden cup." But the maid answered her, and even spoke more haughtily than before, "Drink if you will, but I shall not be your waiting-maid." Then the princess was so thirsty that she got off her horse and lay down, and held her head over the running stream, and cried, and said, "What will become of me?" And the lock of hair answered her again—

> "Alas! alas! if thy mother knew it,
> Sadly, sadly her heart would rue it."

And as she leaned down to drink, the lock of hair fell from her bosom and floated away with the water, without her seeing it, she was so much frightened. But her maid saw it, and was very glad, for she knew the charm, and saw that the poor bride would be in her power now that she had lost the hair. So when the bride had finished drinking, and would have got upon Falada again, the maid said, "I shall ride upon Falada, and you may have my horse instead;" so she was forced to give up her horse, and soon afterwards to take off her royal clothes, and put on her maid's shabby ones.

At last, as they drew near the end of the journey, this treacherous servant threatened to kill her mistress if she ever told anyone what had happened. But Falada saw it all, and marked it well. Then the waiting-maid got upon Falada, and the real bride was set upon the other horse, and they went on in this way till at last they came to the royal court. There was great joy at their coming, and the prince hurried to meet them, and lifted the maid from her horse, thinking she was the one who was to be his wife; and she was led upstairs to the royal chamber, but the true princess was told to stay in the court below.

However, the old king happened to be looking out of the window, and saw her in the yard below; and as she looked very pretty, and too delicate for a waiting-maid, he went into the royal chamber to ask the bride whom it was she had brought with her, that was thus left standing in the court below. "I brought her with me for the sake of her company on the road," said she. "Pray give the girl some work to do, that she may not be idle." The old king could not for some time think of any work for her, but at last he said, "I have a lad who takes care of my geese; she may go and help him." Now the name of this lad, that the real bride was to help in watching the king's geese, was Curdken.

Soon after, the false bride said to the prince, "Dear husband, pray do me one piece of kindness." "That I will," said the prince. "Then tell one of your slaughterers to cut off the head of the horse I rode upon, for it was very unruly, and plagued me sadly on the road." But the truth was, she was very much afraid lest Falada should speak, and tell all she had done to the princess. She carried her point, and the faithful Falada was killed; but when the true princess heard of it she wept, and begged the man to nail up Falada's head against a large dark gate in the city through which she had to pass every morning and evening, that there she might still see him sometimes. Then the slaughterer said he would do as she wished, so he cut off the head and nailed it fast under the dark gate.

Early the next morning, as the princess and Curdken went out through the gate, she said sorrowfully—

"Falada, Falada, there thou art hanging!"

and the head answered—

"Bride, bride, there thou are ganging!
Alas! alas! if thy mother knew it,
Sadly, sadly her heart would rue it."

Then they went out of the city, driving the geese. And when they came to the meadow, the princess sat down upon a bank there and let down her waving locks of hair, which were all of pure gold; and when Curdken saw it glitter in the sun, he ran up, and would have pulled some of the locks out; but she cried—

"Blow, breezes, blow!
Let Curdken's hat go!
Blow breezes, blow!
Let him after it go!

"O'er hills, dales, and rocks,
Away be it whirl'd,
Till the golden locks
Are all comb'd and curl'd!"

Then there came a wind, so strong that it blew off Curdken's hat, and away it flew over the hills, and he after it; till, by the time he came back, she had done combing and curling her hair, and put it up again safely. Then he was very angry and sulky, and would not speak to her at all; but they watched the geese until it grew dark in the evening, and then drove them homewards.

The next morning, as they were going through the dark gate, the poor girl looked up at Falada's head, and cried—

"Falada, Falada, there thou art hanging!"

and it answered—

"Bride, bride, there thou are ganging!
Alas! alas! if thy mother knew it,
Sadly, sadly her heart would rue it."

Then she drove on the geese and sat down again in the meadow, and began to comb out her hair as before, and Curdken ran up to her, and wanted to take of it; but she cried out quickly—

"Blow, breezes, blow!

4

Let Curdken's hat go!
Blow breezes, blow!
Let him after it go!
O'er hills, dales, and rocks,
Away be it whirl'd,
Till the golden locks
Are all comb'd and curl'd!"

Then the wind came and blew off his hat, and off it flew a great distance over the hills and far away, so that he had to run after it: and when he came back, she had done up her hair again, and all was safe. So they watched the geese till it grew dark.

In the evening, after they came home, Curdken went to the old king, and said, "I cannot have that strange girl to help me to keep the geese any longer."

"Why?" inquired the king.

"Because she does nothing but tease me all day long."

Then the king made him tell him all that had passed.

And Curdken said, "When we go in the morning through the dark gate with our flock of geese, she weeps, and talks with the head of a horse that hangs upon the wall, and says—

"Falada, Falada, there thou art hanging!"

and the head answers—

"Bride, bride, there thou are ganging!
Alas! alas! if thy mother knew it,
Sadly, sadly her heart would rue it."

And Curdken went on telling the king what had happened upon the meadow where the geese fed; and how his hat was blown away, and he was forced to run after it, and leave his flock. But the old king told him to go out again as usual the next day: and when morning came, he placed himself behind the dark gate, and heard how the princess spoke, and how Falada answered; and then he went into the field and hid himself in a bush by the meadow's side, and soon saw with his own eyes how they drove the flock of geese, and how, after a little time, she let down her hair that glittered in the sun; and then he heard her say—

"Blow, breezes, blow!
Let Curdken's hat go!
Blow breezes, blow!
Let him after it go!
O'er hills, dales, and rocks,
Away be it whirl'd,

Till the golden locks
Are all comb'd and curl'd!"

And soon came a gale of wind, and carried away Curdken's hat, while the girl went on combing and curling her hair.

All this the old king saw; so he went home without being seen; and when the goose-girl came back in the evening, he called her aside, and asked her why she did so; but she burst into tears, and said, "That I must not tell you or any man, or I shall lose my life."

But the old king begged so hard that she had no peace till she had told him all, word for word: and it was very lucky for her that she did so, for the king ordered royal clothes to be put upon her, and he gazed with wonder, she was so beautiful.

Then he called his son, and told him that he had only the false bride, for that she was merely a waiting-maid, while the true one stood by.

And the young king rejoiced when he saw her beauty, and heard how meek and patient she had been; and without saying anything, he ordered a great feast to be prepared for all his court.

The bridegroom sat at the top, with the false princess on one side, and the true one on the other; but nobody knew her, for she was quite dazzling to their eyes, and was not at all like the little goose-girl, now that she had on her brilliant dress.

When they had eaten and drunk, and were very merry, the old king told all the story, as one that he had once heard of, and asked the true waiting-maid what she thought ought to be done to anyone who would behave thus.

"Nothing better," said this false bride, "than that she should be thrown into a cask stuck around with sharp nails, and that two white horses should be put to it, and should drag it from street to street till she is dead."

"Thou art she!" said the old king; "and since thou hast judged thyself, it shall be so done to thee."

Then the young king was married to his true wife, and they reigned over the kingdom in peace and happiness all their lives.

# THE LITTLE BROTHER AND SISTER

There was once a little brother who took his Sister by the hand, and said, "Since our own dear mother's death we have not had one happy hour; our stepmother beats us every day, and, when we come near her, kicks us away with her foot. Come, let us wander forth into the wide world." So all day long they travelled over meadows, fields, and stony roads. By the evening they came into a large forest, and laid themselves down in a hollow tree, and went to sleep. When they awoke the next morning, the sun had already risen high in the heavens, and its beams made the tree so hot that the little boy said to his sister, "I am so very thirsty, that if I knew where there was a brook, I would go and drink. Ah! I think I hear one running;" and so saying, he got up, and taking his Sister's hand they went to look for the brook.

The wicked stepmother, however, was a witch, and had witnessed the departure of the two children: so, sneaking after them secretly, as is the habit of witches, she had enchanted all the springs in the forest.

Presently they found a brook, which ran trippingly over the pebbles, and the Brother would have drunk out of it, but the Sister heard how it said as it ran along, "Who drinks of me will become a tiger!" So the Sister exclaimed, "I pray you, Brother, drink not, or you will become a tiger, and tear me to pieces!" So the Brother did not drink, although his thirst was very great, and he said, "I will wait till the next brook." As they came to the second, the Sister heard it say, "Who drinks of me becomes a wolf!" The Sister ran up crying, "Brother, do not, pray do not drink, or you will become a wolf and eat me up!" Then the Brother did not drink, saying, "I will wait until we come to the next spring, but then I must drink, you may say what you will; my thirst is much too great." Just as they reached the third brook, the Sister heard the voice saying, "Who drinks of me will become a fawn—who drinks of me will become a fawn!" So the Sister said, "Oh, my Brother do not drink, or you will be changed into a fawn, and run away from me!" But he had already kneeled down, and he drank of the water, and, as the first drops passed his lips, his shape took that of a fawn.

At first the Sister wept over her little, changed Brother, and he wept too, and knelt by her, very sorrowful; but at last the maiden said, "Be still, dear little fawn, and I will never forsake you!" and, taking off her golden garter, she placed it around his neck, and, weaving rushes, made a girdle to lead him with. This she tied to him, and taking the other end in her hand, she led him away, and they travelled deeper and deeper into the forest. After they had gone a long distance they came to a little hut, and the maiden, peeping in, found it empty, and thought, "Here we can stay and dwell." Then she looked for leaves and moss to make a soft couch for the Fawn, and every morning she went out and collected roots and berries and nuts for herself, and tender grass for the Fawn. In the evening when the Sister was tired, and had said her prayers, she laid her head upon the back of the Fawn, which served for a pillow, on which she slept soundly. Had but the Brother regained his own proper form, their lives would have been happy indeed.

7

Thus they dwelt in this wilderness, and some time had elapsed when it happened that the King of the country had a great hunt in the forest; and now sounded through the trees the blowing of horns, the barking of dogs, and the lusty cry of the hunters, so that the little Fawn heard them, and wanted very much to join in. "Ah!" said he to his Sister, "let me go to the hunt, I cannot restrain myself any longer;" and he begged so hard that at last she consented. "But," she told him," "return again in the evening, for I shall shut my door against the wild huntsmen, and, that I may know you, do you knock, and say, 'Sister, dear, let me in,' and if you do not speak I shall not open the door."

As soon as she had said this, the little Fawn sprang off quite glad and merry in the fresh breeze. The King and his huntsmen perceived the beautiful animal, and pursued him; but they could not catch him, and when they thought they certainly had him, he sprang away over the bushes, and got out of sight. Just as it was getting dark, he ran up to the hut, and, knocking, said, "Sister mine, let me in." Then she unfastened the little door, and he went in, and rested all night long upon his soft couch. The next morning the hunt was commenced again, and as soon as the little Fawn heard the horns and the tally-ho of the sportsmen he could not rest, and said, "Sister, dear, open the door; I must be off." The Sister opened it, saying, "Return at evening, mind, and say the words as before." When the King and his huntsmen saw him again, the Fawn with the golden necklace, they followed him, close, but he was too nimble and quick for them. The whole day long they kept up with him, but towards evening the huntsmen made a circle around him, and one wounded him slightly in the hinder foot, so that he could run but slowly. Then one of them slipped after him to the little hut, and heard him say, "Sister, dear, open the door," and saw that the door was opened and immediately shut behind him. The huntsman, having observed all this, went and told the King what he had seen and heard, and he said, "On the morrow I will pursue him once again."

The Sister, however, was terribly afraid when she saw that her Fawn was wounded, and, washing off the blood, she put herbs upon the foot, and said, "Go and rest upon your bed, dear Fawn, that your wound may heal." It was so slight, that the next morning he felt nothing of it, and when he heard the hunting cries outside, he exclaimed, "I cannot stop away—I must be there, and none shall catch me so easily again!" The Sister wept very much and told him, "Soon will they kill you, and I shall be here alone in this forest, forsaken by all the world: I cannot let you go."

"I shall die here in vexation," answered the Fawn, "if you do not, for when I hear the horn, I think I shall jump out of my skin." The Sister, finding she could not prevent him, opened the door, with a heavy heart, and the Fawn jumped out, quite delighted, into the forest. As soon as the King perceived him, he said to his huntsmen, "Follow him all day long till the evening, but let no one do him any harm." Then when the sun had set, the King asked his huntsman to show him the hut; and as they came to it he knocked at the door and said, "Let me in, dear Sister." Upon this the door opened, and, stepping in, the King saw a maiden more beautiful than he had ever beheld before. She was frightened when she saw not her Fawn, but a man enter, who had a golden crown upon his head. But the King, looking at her with a kindly glance, held out to her his hand, saying, "Will you go with me to my castle, and be my dear wife?" "Oh, yes," replied the maiden; "but the Fawn must go too: him I will never forsake." The King replied, "He shall remain with you as long as you live, and shall never want."

The King took the beautiful maiden upon his horse, and rode to his castle, where the wedding was celebrated with great splendor and she became Queen, and they lived together a long time; while the Fawn was taken care of and played about the castle garden.

The wicked stepmother, however, on whose account the children had wandered forth into the world, had supposed that long ago the Sister had been torn into pieces by the wild beasts, and the little Brother in his Fawn's shape hunted to death by the hunters. As soon, therefore, as she heard how happy they had become, and how everything prospered with them, envy and jealousy were aroused in her wicked heart, and left her no peace; and she was always thinking in what way she could bring misfortune upon them.

Her own daughter, who was as ugly as night, and had but one eye, for which she was continually reproached, said, "The luck of being a Queen has never happened to me." "Be quiet, now," replied the old woman, "and make yourself contented: when the time comes I will help and assist you." As soon, then, as the time came when the Queen gave birth to a beautiful little boy, which happened when the King was out hunting, the old witch took the form of a chambermaid, and got into the room where the Queen was lying, and said to her, "The bath is ready, which will restore you and give you fresh strength; be quick before it gets cold." Her daughter being at hand, they carried the weak Queen between them into the room, and laid her in the bath, and then, shutting the door, they ran off; but first they made up an immense fire in the stove, which must soon suffocate the poor young Queen.

When this was done, the old woman took her daughter, and, putting a cap upon her head, laid her in the bed in the Queen's place. She gave her, too, the form and appearance of the real Queen, as far as she was able; but she could not restore the lost eye, and, so that the King might not notice it, she turned her upon that side where there was no eye.

When midnight came, and every one was asleep, the nurse, who sat by herself, wide awake, near the cradle, in the nursery, saw the door open and the true Queen come in. She took the child in her arms, and rocked it a while, and then, shaking up its pillow, laid it down in its cradle, and covered it over again. She did not forget the Fawn, either, but going to the corner where he was, stroked his head, and then went silently out of the door. The nurse asked in the morning of the guards if any one had passed into the castle during the night; but they answered, "No, we have not seen anybody." For many nights afterwards she came constantly, but never spoke a word; and the nurse saw her always, but she would not trust herself to speak about it to any one.

When some time had passed away, the Queen one night began to speak, and said—

10

"How fares my child! how fares my fawn?
Twice more will I come, but never again."

The nurse made no reply; but, when she had disappeared, went to the King, and told him. The King exclaimed, "Oh, mercy! what does this mean?—the next night I will watch myself by the child." So in the evening he went into the nursery, and about midnight the Queen appeared, and said—

"How fares my child! how fares my fawn?
Once more will I come, but never again."

And she nursed the child, as she usually did, and then disappeared. The King dared not speak; but he watched the following night, and this time she said—

"How fares my child! how fares my fawn?
This time have I come, but never again."

At these words the King could hold back no longer, but, springing up, cried, "You can be no other than my dear wife!" Then she answered, "Yes, I am your dear wife;" and at that moment her life was restored by God's mercy, and she was again as beautiful and charming as ever. She told the King the fraud which the witch and her daughter had practised upon him, and he had them both tried, and sentence was pronounced against them. The little Fawn was disenchanted, and received once more his human form; and the Brother and Sister lived happily together to the end of their days.

# HANSEL AND GRETHEL

Once upon a time there dwelt near a large wood a poor woodcutter, with his wife and two children by his former marriage, a little boy called Hansel, and a girl named Grethel. He had little enough to break or bite; and once, when there was a great famine in the land, he could not procure even his daily bread; and as he lay thinking in his bed one evening, rolling about for trouble, he sighed, and said to his wife, "What will become of us? How can we feed our children, when we have no more than we can eat ourselves?"

"Know, then, my husband," answered she, "we will lead them away, quite early in the morning, into the thickest part of the wood, and there make them a fire, and give them each a little piece of bread; then we will go to our work, and leave them alone, so they will not find the way home again, and we shall be freed from them." "No, wife," replied he, "that I can never do. How can you bring your heart to leave my children all alone in the wood, for the wild beasts will soon come and tear them to pieces?"

"Oh, you simpleton!" said she, "then we must all four die of hunger; you had better plane the coffins for us." But she left him no peace till he consented, saying, "Ah, but I shall regret the poor children."

The two children, however, had not gone to sleep for very hunger, and so they overheard what the stepmother said to their father. Grethel wept bitterly, and said to Hansel, "What will become of us?" "Be quiet, Grethel," said he; "do not cry— I will soon help you." And as soon as their parents had fallen asleep, he got up, put on his coat, and, unbarring the back door, slipped out. The moon shone brilliantly, and the white pebbles which lay before the door seemed like silver pieces, they glittered so brightly. Hansel stooped down, and put as many into his pocket as it would hold; and then going back, he said to Grethel, "Be comforted, dear sister, and sleep in peace; God will not forsake us." And so saying, he went to bed again.

The next morning, before the sun arose, the wife went and awoke the two children. "Get up, you lazy things; we are going into the forest to chop wood." Then she gave them each a piece of bread, saying, "There is something for your dinner; do not eat it before the time, for you will get nothing else." Grethel took the bread in her apron, for Hansel's pocket was full of pebbles; and so they all set out upon their way. When they had gone a little distance, Hansel stood still, and peeped back at the house; and this he repeated several times, till his father said, "Hansel, what are you peeping at, and why do you lag behind? Take care, and remember your legs."

"Ah, father," said Hansel, "I am looking at my white cat sitting upon the roof of the house, and trying to say good-bye." "You simpleton!" said the wife, "that is not a cat; it is only the sun shining on the white chimney." But in reality Hansel was not looking at a cat; but every time he stopped, he dropped a pebble out of his pocket upon the path.

When they came to the middle of the forest, the father told the children to collect wood, and he would make them a fire, so that they should not be cold. So Hansel and Grethel gathered together quite a little mountain of twigs. Then they set fire to them; and as the flame burnt up high, the wife said, "Now, you children, lie down near the fire, and rest yourselves, while we go into the forest and chop wood; when we are ready, I will come and call you."

Hansel and Grethel sat down by the fire, and when it was noon, each ate the piece of bread; and because they could hear the blows of an axe, they thought their father was near: but it was not an axe, but a branch which he had bound to a withered tree, so as to be blown to and fro by the wind. They waited so long that at last their eyes closed from weariness, and they fell fast asleep. When they awoke, it was quite dark, and Grethel began to cry, "How shall we get out of the wood?" But Hansel tried to comfort her by saying, "Wait a little while till the moon rises, and then we will quickly find the way." The moon soon shone forth, and Hansel, taking his sister's hand, followed the pebbles, which glittered like new-coined silver pieces, and showed them the path. All night long they walked on, and as day broke they came to their father's house. They knocked at the door, and when the wife opened it, and saw Hansel and Grethel, she exclaimed, "You wicked children! why did you sleep so long in the wood? We thought you were never coming home again." But their father was very glad, for it had grieved his heart to leave them all alone.

Not long afterward there was again great scarcity in every corner of the land; and one night the children overheard their stepmother saying to their father, "Everything is again consumed; we have only half a loaf left, and then the song is ended: the children must be sent away. We will take them deeper into the wood, so that they may not find the way out again; it is the only means of escape for us."

But her husband felt heavy at heart, and thought, "It were better to share the last crust with the children." His wife, however, would listen to nothing that he said, and scolded and reproached him without end.

He who says A must say B too; and he who consents the first time must also the second.

The children, however, had heard the conversation as they lay awake, and as soon as the old people went to sleep Hansel got up, intending to pick up some pebbles as before; but the wife had locked the door, so that he could not get out. Nevertheless, he comforted Grethel, saying, "Do not cry; sleep in quiet; the good God will not forsake us."

Early in the morning the stepmother came and pulled them out of bed, and gave them each a slice of bread, which was still smaller than the former piece. On the way, Hansel broke his in his pocket, and, stooping every now and then, dropped a crumb upon the path. "Hansel, why do you stop and look about?" said the father; "keep in the path." "I am looking at my little dove," answered Hansel, "nodding a good-bye to me." "Simpleton!" said the wife, "that is no dove, but only the sun shining on the chimney." But Hansel still kept dropping crumbs as he went along.

The mother led the children deep into the wood, where they had never been before, and there making an immense fire, she said to them, "Sit down here and rest, and when you feel tired you can sleep for a little while. We are going into the forest to hew wood, and in the evening, when we are ready, we will come and fetch you."

When noon came Grethel shared her bread with Hansel, who had strewn his on the path. Then they went to sleep; but the evening arrived and no one came to visit the poor children, and in the dark night they awoke, and Hansel comforted his sister by saying, "Only wait, Grethel, till the moon comes out, then we shall see the crumbs of bread which I have dropped, and they will show us the way home." The moon shone and they got up, but they could not see any crumbs, for the thousands of birds which had been flying about in the woods and fields had picked them all up. Hansel kept saying to Grethel, "We will soon find the way"; but they did not, and they walked the whole night long and the next day, but still they did not come out of the wood; and they got so hungry, for they had nothing to eat but the berries which they found upon the bushes. Soon they got so tired that they could not drag themselves along, so they lay down under a tree and went to sleep.

It was now the third morning since they had left their father's house, and they still walked on; but they only got deeper and deeper into the wood, and Hansel saw that if help did not come very soon they would die of hunger. At about noonday they saw a beautiful snow-white bird sitting upon a bough, which sang so sweetly that they stood still and listened to it. It soon ceased, and spreading its wings flew off; and they followed it until it arrived at a cottage, upon the roof of which it perched; and when they went close up to it they saw that the cottage was made of bread and cakes, and the window-panes were of clear sugar.

"We will go in there," said Hansel, "and have a glorious feast. I will eat a piece of the roof, and you can eat the window. Will they not be sweet?" So Hansel reached up and broke a piece off the roof, in order to see how it tasted, while Grethel stepped up to the window and began to bite it. Then a sweet voice called out in the room, "Tip-tap, tip-tap, who raps at my door?" and the children answered, "the wind, the wind, the child of heaven"; and they went on eating without interruption. Hansel thought the roof tasted very nice, so he tore off a great piece; while Grethel broke a large round pane out of the window, and sat down quite contentedly. Just then the door opened, and a very old woman, walking upon crutches, came out. Hansel and Grethel were so frightened that they let fall what they had in their hands; but the old woman, nodding her head, said, "Ah, you dear children, what has brought you here? Come in and stop with me, and no harm shall befall you"; and so saying she took them both by the hand, and led them into her cottage. A good meal of milk and pancakes, with sugar, apples, and nuts, was spread on the table, and in the back room were two nice little beds, covered with white, where Hansel and Grethel laid themselves down, and thought themselves in heaven. The old woman behaved very kindly to them, but in reality she was a wicked witch who waylaid children, and built the bread-house in order to entice them in, but as soon as they were in her power she killed them, cooked and ate them, and made a great festival of the day. Witches have red eyes, and cannot see very far; but they have a fine sense of smelling, like wild beasts, so that they know when children approach them. When Hansel and Grethel came near the witch's house she laughed wickedly, saying, "Here come two who shall not escape me." And early in the morning, before they awoke, she went up to them, and saw how lovingly they lay sleeping, with their chubby red cheeks, and she mumbled to herself, "That will be a good bite." Then she took up Hansel with her rough hands, and shut him up in a little cage with a lattice-door; and although he screamed loudly it was of no use. Grethel came next, and, shaking her till she awoke, the witch said, "Get up, you lazy thing, and fetch some water to cook something good for your brother, who must remain in that stall and get fat; when he is fat enough I shall eat him." Grethel began to cry, but it was all useless, for the old witch made her do as she wished. So a nice meal was cooked for Hansel, but Grethel got nothing but a crab's claw.

Every morning the old witch came to the cage and said, "Hansel, stretch out your finger that I may feel whether you are getting fat." But Hansel used to stretch out a bone, and the old woman, having very bad sight, thought it was his finger, and wondered very much that he did not get fatter. When four weeks had passed, and Hansel still kept quite lean, she lost all her patience, and would not wait any longer. "Grethel," she called out in a passion, "get some water quickly; be Hansel fat or lean, this morning I will kill and cook him." Oh, how the poor little sister grieved, as she was forced to fetch the water, and fast the tears ran down her cheeks! "Dear good God, help us now!" she exclaimed. "Had we only been eaten by the wild

15

beasts in the wood, then we should have died together." But the old witch called out, "Leave off that noise; it will not help you a bit."

So early in the morning Grethel was forced to go out and fill the kettle, and make a fire. "First, we will bake, however," said the old woman; "I have already heated the oven and kneaded the dough"; and so saying, she pushed poor Grethel up to the oven, out of which the flames were burning fiercely. "Creep in," said the witch, "and see if it is hot enough, and then we will put in the bread"; but she intended when Grethel got in to shut up the oven and let her bake, so that she might eat her as well as Hansel. Grethel perceived what her thoughts were, and said, "I do not know how to do it; how shall I get in?" "You stupid goose," said she, "the opening is big enough. See, I could even get in myself!" and she got up, and put her head into the oven. Then Grethel gave her a push, so that she fell right in, and then shutting the iron door she bolted it! Oh! how horribly she howled; but Grethel ran away, and left the ungodly witch to burn to ashes.

Now she ran to Hansel, and, opening his door, called out, "Hansel, we are saved; the old witch is dead!" So he sprang out, like a bird out of his cage when the door is opened; and they were so glad that they fell upon each other's neck, and kissed each other over and over again. And now, as there was nothing to fear, they went into the witch's house, where in every corner were caskets full of pearls and precious stones. "These are better than pebbles," said Hansel, putting as many into his pocket as it would hold; while Grethel thought, "I will take some too," and filled her apron full. "We must be off now," said Hansel, "and get out of this enchanted forest." But when they had walked for two hours they came to a large piece of water. "We cannot get over," said Hansel; "I can see no bridge at all." "And there is no boat, either," said Grethel; "but there swims a white duck, and I will ask her to help us over." And she sang:

*"Little Duck, good little Duck,*
Grethel and Hansel, here we stand;
There is neither stile nor bridge,
Take us on your back to land."

So the duck came to them, and Hansel sat himself on, and bade his sister sit behind him. "No," answered Grethel, "that will be too much for the duck; she shall take us over one at a time." This the good little bird did, and when both were happily arrived on the other side, and had gone a little way, they came to a well-known wood, which they knew the better every step they went, and at last they perceived their father's house. Then they began to run, and, bursting into the house, they fell into their father's arms. He had not had one happy hour since he had left the children in the forest; and his wife was dead. Grethel shook her apron, and the pearls and precious stones rolled out upon the floor, and Hansel threw down one handful after the other out of his pocket. Then all their sorrows were ended, and they lived together in great happiness.

My tale is done. There runs a mouse; whoever catches her may make a great, great cap out of her fur.

# OH, IF I COULD BUT SHIVER!

A father had two sons, the elder of whom was forward and clever enough to do almost anything; but the younger was so stupid that he could learn nothing, and when the people saw him they said, "Will thy father still keep thee as a burden to him?" So, if anything was to be done, the elder had at all times to do it; but sometimes the father would call him to fetch something in the dead of night, and perhaps the way led through the churchyard or by a dismal place, and then he used to answer, "No, father, I cannot go there, I am afraid," for he was a coward. Or sometimes of an evening, tales were told by the fireside which made one shudder, and the listeners exclaimed, "Oh, it makes us shiver!" In a corner, meanwhile, sat the younger son, listening, but he could not comprehend what was said, and he thought, "They say continually, 'Oh, it makes us shiver, it makes us shiver!' but perhaps shivering is an art which I cannot understand." One day, however, his father said to him, "Do you hear, you there in the corner? You are growing stout and big; you must learn some trade to get your living by. Do you see how your brother works? But as for you, you are not worth malt and hops."

"Ah, father," answered he, "I would willingly learn something. When shall I begin? I want to know what shivering means, for of that I can understand nothing."

The elder brother laughed when he heard this speech, and thought to himself, "Ah! my brother is such a simpleton that he cannot earn his own living. He who would make a good hedge must learn betimes to bend." But the father sighed and said, "What shivering means you may learn soon enough, but you will never get your bread by that."

Soon after the parish sexton came in for a gossip, so the father told him his troubles, and how that his younger son was such a simpleton that he knew nothing and could learn nothing. "Just fancy, when I asked him how he intended to earn his bread, he desired to learn what shivering meant!" "Oh, if that be all," answered the sexton, "he can learn that soon enough with me; just send him to my place, and I will soon teach him." The father was very glad, because he thought that it would do the boy good; so the sexton took him home to ring the bells. About two days afterward he called him up at midnight to go into the church-tower to toll the bell. "You shall soon learn what shivering means," thought the sexton, and getting up he went out too. As soon as the boy reached the belfry, and turned himself round to seize the rope, he saw upon the stairs, near the sounding-hole, a white figure. "Who's there?" he called out; but the figure gave no answer, and neither stirred nor spoke. "Answer," said the boy, "or make haste off; you have no business here to-night." But the sexton did not stir, so that the boy might think it was a ghost.

The boy called out a second time, "What are you doing here? Speak, if you are an honest fellow, or else I will throw you downstairs."

The sexton said to himself, "That is not a bad thought"; but he remained quiet as if he were a stone. Then the boy called out for the third time, but it produced no effect; so, making a spring, he threw the ghost down the stairs, so that it rolled ten steps, and then lay motionless in a corner. Thereupon he rang the bell, and then going home, he went to bed without saying a word, and fell fast asleep. The sexton's wife waited some time for her husband, but he did not come; so at last she became anxious, woke the boy, and asked him if he knew where her husband was, who had gone before him to the belfry.

"No," answered the boy; "but there was someone standing on the steps who would not give any answer, nor go away, so I took him for a thief and threw him downstairs. Go now and see where he is; perhaps it may be he, but I should be sorry for it." The wife ran off and found her husband lying in a corner, groaning, with one of his ribs broken.

She took him up and ran with loud outcries to the boy's father, and said to him, "Your son has brought a great misfortune on us; he has thrown my husband down and broken his bones. Take the good-for-nothing fellow from our house."

The terrified father came in haste and scolded the boy. "What do these wicked tricks mean? They will only bring misfortune upon you."

"Father," answered the lad, "hear me! I am quite innocent. He stood there at midnight like one who had done some evil; I did not know who it was, and cried three times, 'Speak, or be off!'"

"Ah!" said the father, "everything goes badly with you. Get out of my sight; I do not wish to see you again!"

"Yes, father, willingly; wait but one day, then I will go out and learn what shivering means, that I may at least understand one business which will support me."

"Learn what you will," replied the father, "all is the same to me. Here are fifty dollars; go forth with them into the world, and tell no man whence you came, or who your father is, for I am ashamed of you."

"Yes, father, as you wish; but if you desire nothing else, I shall esteem that very lightly."

As soon as day broke the youth put his fifty dollars into a knapsack and went out upon the high road, saying continually, "Oh, if I could but shiver!"

Presently a man came up, who heard the boy talking to himself; and, as they we're just passing the place where the gallows stood, the man said, "Do you see? There is the tree where seven fellows have married the hempen maid, and now swing to and fro. Sit yourself down there and wait till midnight, and then you will know what it is to shiver!"

"Oh, if that be all," answered the boy, "I can very easily do that! But if I learn so speedily what shivering is, then you shall have my fifty dollars if you come again in the morning."

Then the boy went to the gallows, sat down, and waited for evening, and as he felt cold he made a fire. But about midnight the wind blew so sharp, that in spite of the fire he could not keep himself warm. The wind blew the bodies against one another, so that they swung backward and forward, and he thought, "If I am cold here below by the fire, how must they freeze above!" So his compassion was excited, and, contriving a ladder, he mounted, and, unloosening them one after another, he brought down all seven. Then he poked and blew the fire, and set them round that they might warm themselves; but as they sat still without moving their clothing caught fire. So he said, "Take care of yourselves, or I will hang all of you up again." The dead heard not, and silently allowed their rags to burn. This made him so angry that he said, "If you will not hear I cannot help you; but I will not burn with you." So he hung them up again in a row, and sitting down by the fire he soon went to sleep. The next morning the man came, expecting to receive his fifty dollars, and asked, "Now do you know what shivering means?" "No," he answered; "how should I know? Those fellows up there have not opened their mouths, and were so stupid that they let the old rags on their bodies be burnt." Then the man saw that he should not carry away the fifty dollars that day, so he went away saying, "I never met with such a one before."

The boy also went on his way and began again to say, "Ah, if only I could but shiver—if I could but shiver!" A wagoner walking behind overheard him, and asked, "Who are you?"

"I do not know," answered the boy.

The wagoner asked again, "What do you here?"

20

"I know not."

"Who is your father?"

"I dare not say."

"What is it you are continually grumbling about?"

"Oh," replied the youth, "I wish to learn what shivering is, but nobody can teach me."

"Cease your silly talk," said the wagoner. "Come with me, and I will see what I can do for you." So the boy went with the wagoner, and about evening time they arrived at an inn where they put up for the night, and while they were going into the parlor he said, quite aloud, "Oh, if I could but shiver—if I could but shiver!" The host overheard him and said, laughingly, "Oh, if that is all you wish, you shall soon have the opportunity." "Hold your tongue," said his wife; "so many imprudent people have already lost their lives, it were a shame and sin to such beautiful eyes that they should not see the light again." But the youth said, "If it were ever so difficult I would at once learn it; for that reason I left home"; and he never let the host have any peace till he told him that not far off stood an enchanted castle, where any one might soon learn to shiver if he would watch there three nights. The King had promised his daughter in marriage to whoever would venture, and she was the most beautiful young lady that the sun ever shone upon. And he further told him that inside the castle there was an immense amount of treasure guarded by evil spirits; enough to make any one free, and turn a poor man into a very rich one. Many, he added, had already ventured into this castle, but no one had ever come out again.

The next morning this youth went to the King, and said, "If you will allow me, I wish to watch three nights in the enchanted castle." The King looked at him, and because his appearance pleased him, he said, "You may make three requests, but they must be inanimate things you ask for, and such as you can take with you into the castle." So the youth asked for a fire, a lathe, and a cutting-board.

The King let him take these things by day into the castle, and when it was evening the youth went in and made himself a bright fire in one of the rooms, and, placing his cutting-board and knife near it, he sat down upon his lathe. "Ah, if I could but shiver!" said he. "But even here I shall never learn." At midnight he got up to stir the fire, and, as he poked it, there shrieked suddenly in one corner, "Miau, miau! how cold I am!" "You simpleton!" he exclaimed, "what are you shrieking for? If you are so cold come and sit down by the fire and warm yourself!" As he was speaking, two great black cats sprang up to him with an immense jump and sat down one on each side, looking at him quite wildly with their fiery eyes. When they had warmed themselves for a little while they said, "Comrade, shall we have a game of cards?" "Certainly," he replied; "but let me see your paws first." So they stretched out their claws, and he said, "Ah, what long nails you have got; wait a bit, I must cut them off first"; and so saying he caught them up by the necks, and put them on his board and screwed their feet down. "Since I have seen what you are about I have lost my relish for a game at cards," said he; and, instantly killing them, threw them away into the water. But no sooner had he quieted these two and thought of sitting down again by his fire, than there came out of every hole and corner black cats and black dogs with glowing chains, continually more and more, so that he could not hide himself. They howled fearfully, and jumped upon his fire, and scattered it about as if they would extinguish it. He looked on quietly for some time, but at last, getting angry, he took up his knife and called out, "Away with you, you vagabonds!" and chased them about until a part ran off, and the rest he killed and threw into the pond. As soon as he returned he blew up the sparks of his fire again and warmed himself, and while he sat his eyes began to feel very heavy and he wished to go to sleep. So looking around he saw a great bed in one corner, in which he lay down; but no sooner had he closed his eyes, than the bed began to move of itself and travelled all round the castle. "Just so," said he, "only better still"; whereupon the bed galloped away as if six horses pulled it up and down steps and stairs, until at last, all at once, it overset, bottom upward, and lay upon him like a mountain; but up he got, threw pillows and mattresses into the air, and saying, "Now he who wishes may travel," laid himself down by the fire and slept till day broke. In the morning the King came, and, seeing the youth lying on the ground, he thought that the spectres had killed him, and that he was dead; so he said, "It is a great misfortune that the finest men are thus killed"; but the youth, hearing this, sprang up, saying, "It is not come to that with me yet!" The King was much astonished, but very glad, and asked him how he had fared. "Very well," replied he; "as one night has passed, so also may the other two." Soon after he met his landlord, who opened his eyes when he saw him. "I never thought to see you alive again," said he; "have you learnt now what shivering means?" "No," said he; "it is all of no use. Oh, if any one would but tell me!"

The second night he went up again into the castle, and sitting down by the fire, began his old song, "If I could but shiver!" When midnight came, a ringing and a rattling noise was heard, gentle at first and louder and louder by degrees; then there was a pause, and presently with a loud outcry half a man's body came down the chimney and fell at his feet. "Holloa," he exclaimed; "only half a man answered that ringing; that is too little." Then the ringing began afresh, and a roaring and howling was heard, and the other half fell down. "Wait a bit," said he; "I will poke up the fire first." When he had done so and looked round again, the two pieces had joined themselves together, and an ugly man was sitting in his place. "I did not bargain for that," said the youth; "the bench is mine." The man tried to push him away, but the youth would not let him, and giving him a violent push sat himself down in his old place. Presently more men fell down the chimney, one after the other, who brought nine thigh-bones and two skulls, which they set up, and then they began to play at ninepins. At this the youth wished also to play, so he asked whether he might join them. "Yes, if you have money!" "Money enough," he replied, "but your balls are not quite round"; so saying he took up the skulls, and, placing them on his lathe, turned them round. "Ah, now you will roll well," said he. "Holloa! now we will go at it merrily." So he played with them and lost some of his money, but as it struck twelve everything disappeared. Then he lay down and went to sleep quietly. On the morrow the King came for news, and asked him how he had fared this time. "I have been playing ninepins," he replied, "and lost a couple of dollars." "Have you not shivered?" "No! I have enjoyed myself very much; but I wish some one would teach me that!"

On the third night he sat down again on his bench, saying in great vexation, "Oh, if I could only shiver!" When it grew late, six tall men came in bearing a coffin between them. "Ah, ah," said he, "that is surely my little cousin, who died two days ago"; and beckoning with his finger he called, "Come, little cousin, come!" The men set down the coffin upon the ground, and he went up and took off the lid, and there lay a dead man within, and as he felt the face it was as cold as ice. "Stop a moment," he cried; "I will warm it in a trice"; and stepping up to the fire he warmed his hands, and then laid them upon the face, but it remained cold. So he took up the body, and sitting down by the fire, he laid it on his lap and rubbed the arms that the blood might circulate again. But all this was of no avail, and he thought to himself if two lie in a bed together they warm each other; so he put the body in the bed, and covering it up laid himself down by its side. After a little while the body became warm and began to move about. "See, my cousin," he exclaimed, "have I not warmed you?" But the body got up and exclaimed, "Now I will strangle you." "Is that your gratitude?" cried the youth. "Then you shall get into your coffin again"; and taking it up, he threw the body in, and made the lid fast. Then the six men came in again and bore it away. "Oh, deary me," said he, "I shall never be able to shiver if I stop here all my lifetime!" At these words in came a man who was taller than all the others, and looked more horrible; but he was very old and had a long white beard. "Oh, you wretch," he exclaimed, "now thou shalt learn what shivering means, for thou shalt die!"

"Not so quick," answered the youth; "if I die I must be brought to it first."

"I will quickly seize you," replied the ugly one.

"Softly, softly; be not too sure. I am as strong as you, and perhaps stronger."

"That we will see," said the ugly man. "If you are stronger than I, I will let you go; come, let us try"; and he led him away through a dark passage to a smith's forge. Then taking up an axe he cut through the anvil at one blow down to the ground. "I can do that still better," said the youth, and went to another anvil, while the old man followed him and watched him, with his long beard hanging down. Then the youth took up an axe, and, splitting the anvil at one blow, wedged the old man's beard in it. "Now I have you; now death comes upon you!" and taking up an iron bar he beat the old man until he groaned, and begged him to stop, and he would give him great riches. So the youth drew out the axe, and let him loose. Then the old man, leading him back into the castle, showed him three chests full of gold in a cellar. "One share of this," said he, "belongs to the poor, another to the King, and a third to yourself." And just then it struck twelve and the old man vanished, leaving the youth in the dark. "I must help myself out here," said he, and groping round he found his way back to his room and went to sleep by the fire.

The next morning the King came and inquired, "Now have you learnt to shiver?" "No," replied the youth; "what is it? My dead cousin came here, and a bearded man, who showed me a lot of gold down below; but what shivering means, no one has showed me!" Then the King said, "You have won the castle, and shall marry my daughter."

"That is all very fine," replied the youth, "but still I don't know what shivering means."

So the gold was fetched, and the wedding was celebrated, but the young Prince (for the youth was a Prince now), notwithstanding his love for his bride, and his great contentment, was still continually crying, "If I could but shiver! if I could but shiver!" At last it fell out in this wise: one of the chambermaids said to the Princess, "Let me bring in my aid to teach him what shivering is." So she went to the brook which flowed through the garden, and drew up a pail of water full of little fish; and, at night, when the young Prince was asleep, his bride drew away the covering and poured the pail of cold water and the little fishes over him, so that they slipped all about him. Then the Prince woke up directly, calling out, "Oh! that makes me shiver! dear wife, that makes me shiver! Yes, now I know what shivering means!"

## DUMMLING AND THE THREE FEATHERS

Once upon a time there lived a King who had three sons; the two elder were learned and bright, but the youngest said very little and appeared somewhat foolish, so he was always known as Dummling.

When the King grew old and feeble, feeling that he was nearing his end, he wished to leave the crown to one of his three sons, but could not decide to which. He thereupon settled that they should travel, and that the one who could obtain the most splendid carpet should ascend the throne when he died.

So that there could be no disagreement as to the way each one should go, the King conducted them to the courtyard of the Palace, and there blew three feathers, by turn, into the air, telling his sons to follow the course that the three feathers took.

Then one of the feathers flew eastwards, another westwards, but the third went straight up towards the sky, though it only sped a short distance before falling to earth.

Therefore one son travelled towards the east, and the second went to the west, both making fun of poor Dummling, who was obliged to stay where his feather had fallen. Then Dummling, sitting down and feeling rather miserable after his brothers had gone, looked about him, and noticed that near to where his feather lay was a trap-door. On lifting this up he perceived a flight of steps, down which he went. At the bottom was another door, so he knocked upon it, and then heard a voice calling—

> "Maiden, fairest, come to me,
> Make haste to ope the door,
> A mortal surely you will see,
> From the world above is he,
> We'll help him from our store."

And then the door was flung open, and the young man found himself facing a big toad sitting in the centre of a number of young toads. The big toad addressed him, asking him what he wanted.

Dummling, though rather surprised when he saw the toads, and heard them question him, being good-hearted replied politely—

"I am desirous to obtain the most splendid carpet in the world; just now it would be extremely useful to me."

The toad who had just spoken, called to a young toad, saying—

> "Maiden, fairest, come to me,
> 'Tis a mortal here you see;

Let us speed all his desires,
Giving him what he requires."

Immediately the young toad fetched a large box. This the old one opened, and took out an exquisite carpet, of so beautiful a design, that it certainly could have been manufactured nowhere upon the earth.

Taking it with grateful thanks, Dummling went up the flight of steps, and was once more in the Palace courtyard.

The two elder brothers, being of the opinion that the youngest was so foolish that he was of no account whatever in trying to obtain the throne, for they did not think he would find anything at all, had said to each other:

"It is not necessary for us to trouble much in looking for the carpet!" so they took from the shoulders of the first peasant they came across a coarse shawl, and this they carried to their father.

At the same time Dummling appeared with his beautiful carpet, which he presented to the King, who was very much surprised, and said—

"By rights the throne should be for my youngest son."

But when the two brothers heard this, they gave the old King no rest, saying—

"How is it possible that Dummling, who is not at all wise, could control the affairs of an important kingdom? Make some other condition, we beg of you!"

"Well," agreed the father, "the one who brings me the most magnificent ring shall succeed to my throne," and once more he took his sons outside the Palace. Then, again, he blew three feathers into the air to show the direction each one should go; whereupon the two elder sons went east and west, but Dummling's flew straight up, and fell close by the trap-door. Then the youngest son descended the steps as before, and upon seeing the large toad he talked with her, and told her what he desired. So the big box was brought, and out of it the toad handed him a ring which was of so exquisite a workmanship that no goldsmith's could equal it.

Meanwhile the two elder brothers made fun of the idea of Dummling searching for a ring, and they decided to take no needless trouble themselves.

Therefore, finding an old iron ring belonging to some harness, they took that to the King. Dummling was there before them with his valuable ring, and immediately upon his showing it, the father declared that in justice the kingdom should be his.

In spite of this, however, the two elder sons worried the poor King into appointing one test further, before bestowing his kingdom, and the King, giving way, announced that the one who brought home the most beautiful woman should inherit the crown.

Then Dummling again descended to the large toad and made known to her that he wished to find the most beautiful woman alive.

"The most beautiful woman is not always at hand," said the toad, "however, you shall have her."

Then she gave to him a scooped-out turnip to which half a dozen little mice were attached. The young man regarded this a trifle despondently, for it had no great resemblance to what he was seeking.

"What can I make of this?" he asked.

"Only place in it one of my young toads," replied the large toad, "and then you can decide how to use it."

From the young toads around the old toad, the young man seized one at hazard, and placed it in the scooped-out turnip, but hardly was it there when the most astounding change occurred, for the toad was transformed into a wondrously lovely maiden, the turnip became an elegant carriage, and the six mice were turned into handsome horses. The young man kissed the maiden and drove off to bring her to the King.

Not long afterwards the two brothers arrived.

In the same way, as the twice before, they had taken no trouble about the matter, but had picked up the first passable looking peasant woman whom they had happened to meet.

After glancing at the three, the King said: "Without doubt, at my death the kingdom will be Dummling's."

Once more the brothers loudly expressed their discontent, and gave the King no peace, declaring—

"It is impossible for us to agree to Dummling becoming ruler of the kingdom," and they insisted that the women should be required to spring through a hoop which was suspended from the ceiling in the centre of the hall, thinking to themselves "Now, certainly our peasants will get the best of it, they are active and sturdy, but that fragile lady will kill herself if she jumps."

To this, again, the King consented, and the peasants were first given trial.

They sprang through the hoop, indeed, but so clumsily that they fell, breaking their arms and legs.

Upon which the lovely lady whom Dummling had brought home, leapt through as lightly as a fawn, and this put an end to all contention.

So the crown came to Dummling, who lived long, and ruled his people temperately and justly.

# LITTLE SNOW WHITE

It was in the middle of winter, when the broad flakes of snow were falling around, that a certain queen sat working at her window, the frame of which was made of fine black ebony; and, as she was looking out upon the snow, she pricked her finger, and three drops of blood fell upon it. Then she gazed thoughtfully down on the red drops which sprinkled the white snow and said, "Would that my little daughter may be as white as that snow, as red as the blood, and as black as the ebony window-frame!" And so the little girl grew up; her skin was a white as snow, her cheeks as rosy as blood, and her hair as black as ebony; and she was called Snow-White.

But this queen died; and the king soon married another wife, who was very beautiful, but so proud that she could not bear to think that any one could surpass her. She had a magical looking-glass, to which she used to go and gaze upon herself in it, and say—

> "Tell me, glass, tell me true!
> Of all the ladies in the land,
> Who is fairest? tell me who?"

And the glass answered, "Thou, Queen, art fairest in the land"

But Snow-White grew more and more beautiful; and when she was seven years old, she was as bright as the day, and fairer than the queen herself. Then the glass one day answered queen, when she went to consult it as usual—

> "Thou, Queen, may'st fair and beauteous be,
> But Snow-White is lovelier far than thee?"

When the queen heard this she turned pale with rage and envy; and calling to one of her servants said, "Take Snow-White away into the wide wood, that I may never see her more." Then the servant led the little girl away; but his heart melted when she begged him to spare her life, and he said, "I will not hurt thee, thou pretty child." So he left her there alone; and though he thought it most likely that the wild beasts would tear her to pieces, he felt as if a great weight were taken off his heart when he had made up his mind not to kill her, but leave her to her fate.

Then poor Snow-White wandered along through the wood in great fear; and the wild beasts roared around, but none did her any harm. In the evening she came to a little cottage, and went in there to rest, for her weary feet would carry her no further. Everything was spruce and neat in the cottage: on the table was spread a white cloth, and there were seven little plates with seven little loaves and seven little glasses with wine in them; and knives and forks laid in order, and by the wall stood seven little beds. Then, as she was exceedingly hungry, she picked a little piece off each loaf, and drank a very little wine out of each glass; and after that she thought she would lie down and rest. So she tried all the little beds; and one was too long, and another was too short, till, at last, the seventh suited her; and there she laid herself down and went to sleep. Presently in came the masters of the cottage, who were seven little dwarfs that lived among the mountains, and dug and searched about for gold. They lighted up their seven lamps, and saw directly that all was not right. The first said, "Who has been sitting on my stool?" The second, "Who has been eating off my plate?" The third, "Who has been picking at my bread?" The fourth, "Who has been meddling with my spoon?" The fifth, "Who has been handling my fork?" The sixth, "Who has been cutting with my knife?" The seventh, "Who has been drinking my wine?" Then the first looked around and said, "Who has been lying on my bed?" And the rest came running to him, and every one cried out that somebody had been upon his bed. But the seventh saw Snow-White, and called upon his brethren to come and look at her; and they cried out with wonder and astonishment, and brought their lamps and gazing upon her, they said, "Good heavens! what a lovely child she is!" And they were delighted to see her, and took care not to waken her; and the seventh dwarf slept an hour with each of the other dwarfs in turn, till the night was gone.

In the morning Snow-White told them all her story, and they pitied her, and said if she would keep all things in order, and cook and wash, and knit and spin for them, she might stay where she was, and they would take good care of her. Then they went out all day long to their work, seeking for gold and silver in the mountains; and Snow-White remained at home; and they warned her, saying, "The queen will soon find out where you are, so take care and let no one in." But the queen, now that she thought Snow-White was dead, believed that she was certainly the handsomest lady in the land; so she went to her glass and said—

> "Tell me, glass, tell me true!
> Of all the ladies in the land,
> Who is fairest? tell me who?"

And the glass answered—

> "Thou, Queen, thou are fairest in all this land;
> But over the Hills, in the greenwood shade,
> Where the seven dwarfs their dwelling have made,
> There Snow-White is hiding; and she
> Is lovelier far, O Queen, than thee."

Then the queen was very much alarmed; for she knew that the glass always spoke the truth, and she was sure that the servant had betrayed her. And as she could not bear to think that any one lived who was more beautiful than she was, she disguised herself as an old pedlar woman and went her way over the hills to the place where the dwarfs dwelt. Then she knocked at the door and cried, "Fine wares to sell!" Snow-White looked out of the window, and said, "Good day, good woman; what have you to sell?" "Good wares, fine wares," replied she; "laces and bobbins of all colors." "I will let the old lady in; she seems to be a very good sort of a body," thought Snow-White; so she ran down, and unbolted the door. "Bless me!" said the woman, "how badly your stays are laced. Let me lace them up with one of my nice new laces." Snow-White did not dream of any mischief; so she stood up before the old woman who set to work so nimbly, and pulled the lace so tightly that Snow-White lost her breath, and fell down as if she were dead. "There's an end of all thy beauty," said the spiteful queen, and went away home.

In the evening the seven dwarfs returned; and I need not say how grieved they were to see their faithful Snow-White stretched upon the ground motionless, as if she were quite dead. However, they lifted her up, and when they found what was the matter, they cut the lace; and in a little time she began to breathe, and soon came to herself again. Then they said, "The old woman was the queen; take care another time, and let no one in when we are away."

When the queen got home, she went to her glass, and spoke to it, but to her surprise it replied in the same words as before.

Then the blood ran cold in her heart with spite and malice to hear that Snow-White still lived; and she dressed herself up again in a disguise, but very different from the one she wore before, and took with her a poisoned comb. When she reached the dwarfs' cottage, she knocked at the door, and cried, "Fine wares to sell!" but Snow-White said, "I dare not let any one in." Then the queen said, "Only look at my beautiful combs;" and gave her the poisoned one. And it looked so pretty that the little girl took it up and put it into her hair to try it; but the moment it touched her head the poison was so powerful that she fell down senseless. "There you may lie," said the queen, and went her way. But by good luck the dwarfs returned very early that evening; and when they saw Snow-White lying on the ground, they thought what had happened, and soon found the poisoned comb. And when they took it away, she recovered, and told them all that had passed; and they warned her once more not to open the door to any one.

Meantime the queen went home to her glass, and trembled with rage when she received exactly the same answer as before; and she said, "Snow-White shall die, if it costs me my life." So she went secretly into a chamber, and prepared a poisoned apple: the outside looked very rosy and tempting, but whosoever tasted it was sure to die. Then she dressed herself up as a peasant's wife, and travelled over the hills to the dwarfs' cottage, and knocked at the door; but Snow-White put her head out of the window, and said, "I dare not let any one in, for the dwarfs have told me not to." "Do as you please," said the old woman, "but at any rate take this pretty apple; I will make you a present of it." "No," said Snow-White, "I dare not take it." "You silly girl!" answered the other, "what are you afraid of? do you think it is poisoned? Come! do you eat one part, and I will eat the other." Now the apple was so prepared that one side was good, though the other side was poisoned. Then Snow-White was very much tempted to taste, for the apple looked exceedingly nice; and when she saw the old woman eat, she could refrain no longer. But she had scarcely put the piece into her mouth when she fell down dead upon the ground. "This time nothing will save thee," said the queen; and she went home to her glass, and at last it said—"Thou, Queen, art the fairest of all the fair." And then her envious heart was glad, and as happy as such a heart could be.

When evening came, and the dwarfs returned home, they found Snow-White lying on the ground; no breath passed her lips, and they were afraid that she was quite dead. They lifted her up, and combed her hair, and washed her face with wine and water; but all was in vain. So they laid her down upon a bier, and all seven watched and bewailed her three whole days; and then they proposed to bury her; but her cheeks were still rosy, and her face looked just as it did while she was alive; so they said, "We will never bury her in the cold ground." And they made a coffin of glass so that they might still look at her, and wrote her name upon it in golden letters, and that she was a king's daughter. Then the coffin was placed upon the hill, and one of the dwarfs always sat by it and watched. And the birds of the air came, too, and bemoaned Snow-White. First of all came an owl, and then a raven, but at last came a dove.

And thus Snow-White lay for a long, long time, and still only looked as though she were asleep; for she was even now as white as snow, and as red as blood, and as black as ebony. At last a prince came and called at the dwarfs' house; and he saw Snow-White and read what was written in golden letters. Then he offered the dwarfs money, and earnestly prayed them to let him take her away; but they said, "We will not part with her for all the gold in the world." At last, however, they had pity on him, and gave him the coffin; but the moment he lifted it up to carry it home with him, the piece of apple fell from between her lips, and Snow-White awoke, and exclaimed, "Where am I!" And the prince answered, "Thou art safe with me." Then he told her all that had happened, and said, "I love you better than all the world; come with me to my father's palace, and you shall be my wife." Snow-White consented, and went home with the prince; and everything was prepared with great pomp and splendor for their wedding.

To the feast was invited, among the rest, Snow-White's old enemy, the queen; and as she was dressing herself in fine, rich clothes, she looked in the glass and said, "Tell me, glass, tell me true! Of all the ladies in the land, Who is fairest? tell me who?" And the glass answered, "Thou, lady, art the loveliest *here*, I ween; But lovelier far is the new-made queen."

When she heard this, the queen started with rage; but her envy and curiosity were so great, that she could not help setting out to see the bride. And when she arrived, and saw that it was no other than Snow-White, whom she thought had been dead a long while, she choked with passion, and fell ill and died; but Snow-White and the prince lived and reigned happily over that land, many, many years.

# CATHERINE AND FREDERICK

Once upon a time there was a youth named Frederick and a girl called Catherine, who had married and lived together as a young couple. One day Fred said, "I am now going into the fields, dear Catherine, and by the time I return let there be something hot upon the table, for I shall be hungry, and something to drink, too, for I shall be thirsty."

"Very well, dear Fred," said she, "go at once, and I will make all right for you."

As soon, then, as dinner-time approached, she took down a sausage out of the chimney, and putting it in a frying-pan with batter, set it over the fire. Soon the sausage began to frizzle and spit while Catherine stood by holding the handle of the pan and thinking; and among other things she thought that while the sausage was getting ready she might go into the cellar and draw some beer. So she took a can and went down into the cellar to draw the beer, and while it ran into the can, she bethought herself that perhaps the dog might steal the sausage out of the pan, and so up the cellar stairs she ran, but too late, for the rogue had already got the meat in his mouth and was sneaking off. Catherine, however, pursued the dog for a long way over the fields, but the beast was quicker than she, and would not let the sausage go, but bolted off at a great rate. "Off is off!" said Catherine, and turned round, and being very tired and hot, she went home slowly to cool herself. All this while the beer was running out of the cask, for Catherine had forgotten to turn the tap off, and so, as soon as the can was full, the liquor ran over the floor of the cellar until it was all out. Catherine saw the misfortune at the top of the steps. "My gracious!" she exclaimed; "what shall I do that Fred may not find this out?" She considered for some time till she remembered that a sack of fine malt yet remained from the last brewing, in one corner, which she would fetch down and strew about in the beer. "Yes," said she, "it was spared at the right time to be useful to me now in my necessity"; and down she pulled the sack so hastily that she overturned the can of beer for Fred, and away it mixed with the rest on the floor. "It is all right," said she, "where one is, the other should be," and she strewed the malt over the whole cellar. When it was done she was quite overjoyed at her work, and said, "How clean and neat it does look, to be sure!"

At noontime Fred returned. "Now, wife, what have you ready for me?" said he. "Ah, my dear Fred," she replied, "I would have fried you a sausage, but while I drew the beer the dog stole it out of the pan, and while I hunted the dog the beer all ran out, and as I was about to dry up the beer with the malt I overturned your can; but be contented, the cellar is quite dry again now."

"Oh, Catherine, Catherine!" said Fred; "you should not have done so! to let the sausage be stolen! and the beer run out! and over all to shoot our best sack of malt!"

"Well, Fred," said she, "I did not know that; you should have told me."

But the husband thought to himself, if one's wife acts so, one must look after things oneself. Now, he had collected a tolerable sum of silver dollars, which he changed into gold, and then

37

he told his wife, "Do you see, these are yellow counters which I will put in a pot and bury in the stable under the cow's stall; but mind that you do not meddle with it, or you will come to some harm."

Catherine promised to mind what he said, but as soon as Fred was gone some hawkers came into the village with earthenware for sale, and amongst others they asked her if she would purchase anything. "Ah, good people," said Catherine, "I have no money, and cannot buy anything, but if you can make use of yellow counters I will buy them."

"Yellow counters! ah! why not? Let us look at them," said they.

"Go into the stable," she replied, "and dig under the cows stall, and there you will find the yellow counters. I dare not go myself."

The rogues went at once, and soon dug up the shining gold which they quickly pocketed, and then they ran off, leaving behind them their pots and dishes in the house. Catherine thought she might as well make use of the new pottery, and since she had no need of anything in the kitchen, she set out each pot on the ground, and then put others on the top of the palings round the house for ornament. When Fred returned, and saw the fresh decorations, he asked Catherine what she had done. "I have bought them, Fred," said she, "with the yellow counters which lay under the cow's stall; but I did not dig them up myself; the pedlars did that."

"Ah, wife, what have you done?" replied Fred. "They were not counters, but bright gold, which was all the property we possessed: you should not have done so."

38

"Well, dear Fred," replied his wife, "you should have told me so before. I did not know that."

Catherine stood considering for awhile, and presently she began, "Come, Fred, we will soon get the gold back again; let us pursue the thieves."

"Well, come along," said Fred; "we will try at all events; but take butter and cheese with you, that we may have something to eat on our journey."

"Yes, Fred," said she, and soon made herself ready; but, her husband being a good walker, she lagged behind. "Ah!" said she, "this is my luck, for when we turn back I shall be a good bit forward." Presently she came to a hill, on both sides of which there were very deep ruts. "Oh, see!" said she, "how the poor earth is torn, flayed, and wounded; it will never be well again all its life!" And out of compassion she took out her butter, and greased the ruts over right and left, so that the wheels might run more easily through them, and, while she stooped in doing this, a cheese rolled out of her pocket down the mountain. Catherine said when she saw it, "I have already once made the journey up, and I am not coming down after you: another shall run and fetch you." So saying, she took another cheese out of her pocket and rolled it down; but as it did not return, she thought, "Perhaps they are waiting for a companion and don't like to come alone"; and down she bowled a third cheese. Still all three stayed, and she said, "I cannot think what this means; perhaps it is that the third cheese has missed his way: I will send a fourth, that he may call him as he goes by." But this one acted no better than the others, and Catherine became so anxious that she threw down a fifth and a sixth cheese also, and they were the last. For a long time after this she waited, expecting they would come, but when she found they did not she cried out, "You are nice fellows to send after a dead man! you stop a fine time! but do you think I shall wait for you? Oh, no! I shall go on; you can follow me; you have younger legs than I."

So saying, Catherine walked on and came up with Fred, who was waiting for her, because he needed something to eat. "Now," said he, "give me quickly what you brought." She handed him the dry bread. "Where are the butter and cheese?" cried her husband. "Oh, Fred, dear," she replied, "with the butter I have smeared the ruts, and the cheeses will soon come, but one ran away, and I sent the others after it to call it back!"

"It was silly of you to do so," said Fred, "to grease the roads with butter, and to roll cheese down the hill!"

"If you had but told me so," said Catherine, vexedly.

So they ate the dry bread together, and presently Fred said, "Catherine, did you make things fast at home before you came out?"

"No, Fred," said she, "you did not tell me."

"Then go back and lock up the house before we go farther; bring something to eat with you, and I will stop here for you."

Back went Catherine, thinking, "Ah! Fred will like something else to eat. Butter and cheese will not please; I will bring with me a bag of dried apples and a mug of vinegar to drink." When she had put these things together she bolted the upper half of the door, but the under door she raised up and carried away on her shoulder, thinking that certainly the house was well protected if she took such good care of the door! Catherine walked along now very leisurely, for, said she to herself, "Fred will have all the longer rest!" and as soon as she reached him she gave him the door, saying, "There, Fred, now you have the house door you can take care of the house yourself."

"Oh! my goodness," exclaimed the husband, "what a clever wife I have! She has bolted the top door, but brought away the bottom part, where any one can creep through! Now it is too late to go back to the house, but since you brought the door here you may carry it onward."

"The door I will willingly carry," replied Catherine, "but the apples and the vinegar will be too heavy, so I shall hang them on the door and make that carry them!"

Soon after they came into a wood and looked about for the thieves, but they, could not find them, and when it became dark they climbed up into a tree to pass the night. But scarcely had they done this when up came the fellows who carried away what should not go with them, and find things before they are lost. They laid themselves down right under the tree upon which Fred and Catherine were, and making a fire, prepared to share their booty. Then Fred slipped down on the other side, and collected stones, with which he climbed the tree again, to beat the thieves with. The stones, however, did them no harm, for the fellows

40

called out, "Ah! it will soon be morning, for the wind is shaking down the chestnuts." All this while Catherine still had the door upon her shoulder, and, as it pressed very heavily, she thought the dried apples were in fault, and said to Fred, "I must throw down these apples." "No, Catherine," said he, "not now, they might discover us." "Ah, I must, though, they are so heavy."

"Well, then, do it in the hangman's name!" cried Fred.

As they fell down the rogues said, "Ah! the birds are pulling off the leaves."

A little while after Catherine said again, "Oh! Fred, I must pour out the vinegar, it is so heavy."

"No, no!" said he, "it will discover us."

"Ah! but I must, Fred, it is very heavy," said Catherine.

"Well, then, do it in the hangman's name!" cried Fred.

So she poured out the vinegar, and as it dropped on them the thieves said, "Ah! the dew is beginning to fall."

Not many minutes after Catherine found the door was still quite as heavy, and said again to Fred, "Now I must throw down this door."

"No, Catherine," said he, "that would certainly discover us."

"Ah! Fred, but I must; it presses me so terribly."

"No, Catherine dear! do hold it fast," said Fred.

"There—it is gone!" said she.

"Then let it go in the hangman's name!" cried Fred, while it fell crashing through the branches. The rogues below thought the Evil One was descending the tree, and ran off, leaving everything behind them. And early in the morning Fred and his wife descended, and found all their gold under the tree.

As soon as they got home again, Fred said, "Now, Catherine, you must be very industrious and work hard."

"Yes, my dear husband," said she; "I will go into the fields to cut corn." When she was come into the field she said to herself, "Shall I eat before I cut, or sleep first before I cut?" She determined to eat, and soon became so sleepy over her meal that when she began to cut she knew not what she was doing, and cut off half her clothes—gown, petticoat and all. When, after a long sleep, Catherine awoke, she got up half-stripped, and said to herself, "Am I myself? or am I not? Ah! I am not myself." By and by night came on, and Catherine ran into the village, and, knocking at her husband's window, called, "Fred!"

"What is the matter?" cried he.

"I want to know if Catherine is indoors!" said she.

"Yes, yes!" answered Fred, "she is certainly within, fast asleep."

"Then I am at home," said she, and ran away.

Standing outside Catherine found some thieves, wanting to steal, and going up to them she said, "I will help you."

At this the thieves were very glad, not doubting but that she knew where to light on what they sought. But Catherine, stepping in front of the houses, called out, "Good people, what have you that we can steal?" At this the thieves said, "You will do for us with a vengeance!" and they wished they had never come near her; but in order to rid themselves of her they said, "Just before the village the parson has some roots lying in his field; go and fetch some."

Catherine went as she was bid, and began to grub for them, and soon made herself very dirty with the earth. Presently a man came by and saw her, and stood still, for he thought it was the Evil One who was grovelling so among the roots. Away he ran into the village to the parson, and told him the Evil One was in his field, rooting up the turnips. "Ah! heavens!" said the parson, "I have a lame foot, and I cannot go out to exorcize him."

"Then I will carry you a-pickaback," said the man, and took him up.

Just as they arrived in the field, Catherine got up and drew herself up to her full height.

"Oh! it is the Evil One!" cried the parson, and both he and the man hurried away; and, behold! the parson ran faster with his lame legs, through fear and terror, than the countryman could with his sound legs!

## THE VALIANT LITTLE TAILOR

One fine day a Tailor was sitting on his bench by the window in very high spirits, sewing away most diligently, and presently up the street came a country woman, crying, "Good jams for sale! Good jams for sale!" This cry sounded nice in the Tailor's ears, and, poking his diminutive head out of the window, he called, "Here, my good woman, just bring your jams in here!" The woman mounted the three steps up to the Tailor's house with her large basket, and began to open all the pots together before him. He looked at them all, held them up to the light, smelt them, and at last said, "These jams seem to me to be very nice, so you may weigh me out two ounces, my good woman; I don't object even if you make it a quarter of a pound." The woman, who hoped to have met with a good customer, gave him all he wished, and went off grumbling, and in a very bad temper.

"Now!" exclaimed the Tailor, "Heaven will send me a blessing on this jam, and give me fresh strength and vigor;" and, taking the bread from the cupboard, he cut himself a slice the size of the whole loaf, and spread the jam upon it. "That will taste very nice," said he; "but, before I take a bite, I will just finish this waistcoat." So he put the bread on the table and stitched away, making larger and larger stitches every time for joy. Meanwhile the smell of the jam rose to the ceiling, where many flies were sitting, and enticed them down, so that soon a great swarm of them had pitched on the bread. "Holloa! who asked you?" exclaimed the Tailor, driving away the uninvited visitors; but the flies, not understanding his words, would not be driven off, and came back in greater numbers than before. This put the little man in a great passion, and, snatching up in his anger a bag of cloth, he brought it down with a merciless swoop upon them. When he raised it again he counted as many as seven lying dead before him with outstretched legs. "What a fellow you are!" said he to himself, astonished at his own bravery. "The whole town must hear of this." In great haste he cut himself out a band, hemmed it, and then put on it in large letters, "SEVEN AT ONE BLOW!" "Ah," said he, "not one city alone, the whole world shall hear it!" and his heart danced with joy, like a puppy-dog's tail.

The little Tailor bound the belt around his body, and made ready to travel forth into the wide world, feeling the workshop too small for his great deeds. Before he set out, however, he looked about his house to see if there were anything he could carry with him, but he found only an old cheese, which he pocketed, and observing a bird which was caught in the bushes before the door, he captured it, and put that in his pocket also. Soon after he set out boldly on his travels; and, as he was light and active, he felt no fatigue. His road led him up a hill, and when he arrived at the highest point of it he found a great Giant sitting there, who was gazing about him very composedly.

But the little Tailor went boldly up, and said, "Good day, friend; truly you sit there and see the whole world stretched below you. I also am on my way thither to seek my fortune. Are you willing to go with me?"

The Giant looked with scorn at the little Tailor, and said, "You rascal! you wretched creature!"

"Perhaps so," replied the Tailor; "but here may be seen what sort of a man I am;" and, unbuttoning his coat, he showed the Giant his belt. The Giant read, "SEVEN AT ONE BLOW"; and supposing they were men whom the Tailor had killed, he felt some respect for him. Still he meant to try him first; so taking up a pebble, he squeezed it so hard that water dropped out of it. "Do as well as that," said he to the other, "if you have the strength."

"If it be nothing harder than that," said the Tailor, "that's child's play." And, diving into his pocket, he pulled out the cheese and squeezed it till the whey ran out of it, and said, "Now, I fancy that I have done better than you."

The Giant wondered what to say, and could not believe it of the little man; so, catching up another pebble, he flung it so high that it almost went out of sight, saying, "There, you pigmy, do that if you can."

"Well done," said the Tailor; "but your pebble will fall down again to the ground. I will throw one up which will not come down;" and, dipping into his pocket, he took out the bird and threw it into the air. The bird, glad to be free, flew straight up, and then far away, and did not come back. "How does that little performance please you, friend?" asked the Tailor.

"You can throw well," replied the giant; "now truly we will see if you are able to carry something uncommon." So saying, he took him to a large oak tree, which lay upon the ground, and said, "If you are strong enough, now help me to carry this tree out of the forest."

"With pleasure," replied the Tailor; "you may hold the trunk upon your shoulder, and I will lift the boughs and branches, they are the heaviest, and carry them."

The Giant took the trunk upon his shoulder, but the Tailor sat down on one of the branches, and the Giant, who could not look round, was compelled to carry the whole tree and the Tailor also. He being behind, was very cheerful, and laughed at the trick, and presently began to sing the song, "There rode three tailors out at the gate," as if the carrying of trees were a trifle. The Giant, after he had staggered a very short distance with his heavy load, could go no further, and called out, "Do you hear? I must drop the tree." The Tailor, jumping down, quickly embraced the tree with both arms, as if he had been carrying it, and said to the Giant, "Are you such a big fellow, and yet cannot you carry a tree by yourself?"

Then they travelled on further, and as they came to a cherry-tree, the Giant seized the top of the tree where the ripest cherries hung, and, bending it down, gave it to the Tailor to hold, telling him to eat. But the Tailor was far too weak to hold the tree down, and when the Giant let go, the tree flew up in the air, and the Tailor was taken with it. He came down on the other side, however, unhurt, and the Giant said, "What does that mean? Are you not strong enough to hold that twig?" "My strength did not fail me," said the Tailor; "do you imagine that that was a hard task for one who has slain seven at one blow? I sprang over the tree simply because the hunters were shooting down here in the thicket. Jump after me if you can." The Giant made the attempt, but could not clear the tree, and stuck fast in the branches; so that in this affair, too, the Tailor had the advantage.

Then the Giant said, "Since you are such a brave fellow, come with me to my house, and stop a night with me." The Tailor agreed, and followed him; and when they came to the cave, there sat by the fire two other Giants, each with a roast sheep in his hand, of which he was eating. The Tailor sat down thinking. "Ah, this is very much more like the world than is my workshop." And soon the Giant pointed out a bed where he could lie down and go to sleep. The bed, however, was too large for him, so he crept out of it, and lay down in a corner. When midnight came, and the Giant fancied the Tailor would be in a sound sleep, he got up, and taking a heavy iron bar, beat the bed right through at one stroke, and believed he had thereby given the Tailor his death-blow. At the dawn of day the Giants went out into the forest, quite forgetting the Tailor, when presently up he came, quite cheerful, and showed himself before them. The Giants were frightened, and, dreading he might kill them all, they ran away in a great hurry.

The Tailor travelled on, always following his nose, and after he had journeyed some long distance, he came into the courtyard of a royal palace; and feeling very tired he laid himself down on the ground and went to sleep. Whilst he lay there the people came and viewed him on all sides, and read upon his belt, "Seven at one blow." "Ah," they said, "what does this great warrior here in time of peace? This must be some valiant hero." So they went and told the King, knowing that, should war break out, here was a valuable and useful man, whom one ought not to part with at any price. The King took advice, and sent one of his courtiers to the Tailor to beg for his fighting services, if he should be awake. The messenger stopped at the sleeper's side, and waited till he stretched out his limbs and unclosed his eyes, and then he mentioned to him his message. "Solely for that reason did I come here," was his answer; "I am quite willing to enter into the King's service." Then he was taken away with great honor, and a fine house was appointed him to dwell in.

The courtiers, however, became jealous of the Tailor, and wished him at the other end of the world. "What will happen?" said they to one another. "If we go to war with him, when he strikes out seven will fall at one stroke, and nothing will be left for us to do." In their anger they came to the determination to resign, and they went all together to the King, and asked his permission, saying, "We are not prepared to keep company with a man who kills seven at one blow." The King was sorry to lose all his devoted servants for the sake of one, and wished that he had never seen the Tailor, and would gladly have now been rid of him. He dared not, however dismiss him, because he feared the Tailor might kill him and all his subjects, and seat himself upon the throne. For a long time he deliberated, till finally he came to a decision; and, sending for the Tailor, he told him that, seeing he was so great a hero, he wished to beg a favor of him. "In a certain forest in my kingdom," said the King, "there are two Giants, who, by murder, rapine, fire, and robbery, have committed great damage, and no one approaches them without endangering his own life. If you overcome and slay both these Giants, I will give you my only daughter in marriage, and half of my kingdom for a dowry: a hundred knights shall accompany you, too, in order to render you assistance."

"Ah, that is something for a man like me," thought the Tailor to himself: "a lovely Princess and half a kingdom are not offered to one every day." "Oh, yes," he replied, "I will soon settle these two Giants, and a hundred horsemen are not needed for that purpose; he who kills seven at one blow has no fear of two."

Speaking thus, the little Tailor set out, followed by the hundred knights, to whom he said, immediately they came to the edge of the forest, "You must stay here; I prefer to meet these Giants alone."

Then he ran off into the forest, peering about him on all sides; and after a while he saw the two Giants sound asleep under a tree, snoring so loudly that the branches above them shook violently. The Tailor, bold as a lion, filled both his pockets with stones and climbed up the tree. When he got to the middle of it he crawled along a bough, so that he sat just above the sleepers, and then he let fall one stone after another upon the body of one of them. For some time the Giant did not move, until, at last awaking, he pushed his companion, and said, "Why are you hitting me?"

"You have been dreaming," he answered; "I did not touch you." So they laid themselves down again to sleep, and presently the Tailor threw a stone down upon the other. "What is that?" he cried. "Why are you knocking me about?"

"I did not touch you; you are dreaming," said the first. So they argued for a few minutes; but, both being very weary with the day's work, they soon went to sleep again. Then the Tailor began his fun again, and, picking out the largest stone, threw it with all his strength upon the chest of the first Giant. "This is too bad!" he exclaimed; and, jumping up like a madman, he fell upon his companion, who considered himself equally injured, and they set to in such good earnest, that they rooted up trees and beat one another about until they both fell dead upon the ground. Then the Tailor jumped down, saying, "What a piece of luck they did not pull up the tree on which I sat, or else I must have jumped on another like a squirrel, for I am not used to flying." Then he drew his sword, and, cutting a deep wound in the breast of both, he went to the horsemen and said, "The deed is done; I have given each his death-stroke; but it was a tough job, for in their defence they uprooted trees to protect themselves with; still, all that is of no use when such an one as I come, who slew seven at one stroke."

"And are you not wounded?" they asked.

"How can you ask me that? they have not injured a hair of my head," replied the little man. The knights could hardly believe him, till, riding into the forest, they found the Giants lying dead, and the uprooted trees around them.

48

Then the Tailor demanded the promised reward of the King; but he repented of his promise, and began to think of some new plan to shake off the hero. "Before you receive my daughter and the half of my kingdom," said he to him, "you must execute another brave deed. In the forest there lives a unicorn that commits great damage, you must first catch him."

"I fear a unicorn less than I did two Giants! Seven at one blow is my motto," said the Tailor. So he carried with him a rope and an axe and went off to the forest, ordering those, who were told to accompany him, to wait on the outskirts. He had not to hunt long, for soon the unicorn approached, and prepared to rush at him as if it would pierce him on the spot. "Steady! steady!" he exclaimed, "that is not done so easily"; and, waiting till the animal was close upon him, he sprang nimbly behind a tree. The unicorn, rushing with all its force against the tree, stuck its horn so fast in the trunk that it could not pull it out again, and so it remained prisoner.

"Now I have got him," said the Tailor; and coming from behind the tree, he first bound the rope around its neck, and then cutting the horn out of the tree with his axe, he arranged everything, and, leading the unicorn, brought it before the King.

The King, however, would not yet deliver over the promised reward, and made a third demand, that, before the marriage, the Tailor should capture a wild boar which did much damage, and he should have the huntsmen to help him. "With pleasure," was the reply; "it is a mere nothing." The huntsmen, however, he left behind, to their great joy, for this wild boar had already so often hunted them, that they saw no fun in now hunting it. As soon as the boar perceived the Tailor, it ran at him with gaping mouth and glistening teeth, and tried to throw him down on the ground; but our flying hero sprang into a little chapel which stood near, and out again at a window, on the other side, in a moment. The boar ran after him, but he, skipping around, closed the door behind it, and there the furious beast was caught, for it was much too unwieldy and heavy to jump out of the window.

The Tailor now ordered the huntsmen up, that they might see his prisoner with their own eyes; but our hero presented himself before the King, who was obliged at last, whether he would or no, to keep his word, and surrender his daughter and the half of his kingdom.

If he had known that it was no warrior, but only a Tailor, who stood before him, it would have grieved him still more.

So the wedding was celebrated with great magnificence, though with little rejoicing, and out of a Tailor there was made a King.

A short time afterwards the young Queen heard her husband talking in his sleep, saying, "Boy, make me a coat, and then stitch up these trowsers, or I will lay the yard-measure over your shoulders!" Then she understood of what condition her husband was, and complained in the morning to her father, and begged he would free her from her husband, who was nothing more than a tailor. The King comforted her by saying, "This night leave your chamber-door open: my servants shall stand outside, and when he is asleep they shall come in, bind him, and carry him away to a ship, which shall take him out into the wide world." The wife was pleased with the proposal; but the King's armor-bearer, who had overheard all, went to the young King and revealed the whole plot. "I will soon put an end to this affair," said the valiant little Tailor. In the evening at their usual time they went to bed, and when his wife thought he slept she got up, opened the door, and laid herself down again.

The Tailor, however, only pretended to be asleep, and began to call out in a loud voice, "Boy, make me a coat, and then stitch up these trowsers, or I will lay the yard-measure about your shoulders. Seven have I slain with one blow, two Giants have I killed, a unicorn have I led captive, and a wild boar have I caught, and shall I be afraid of those who stand outside my room?"

When the men heard these words spoken by the Tailor, a great fear came over them, and they ran away as if wild huntsmen were following them; neither afterwards dared any man venture to oppose him. Thus the Tailor became a King, and so he lived for the rest of his life.

# LITTLE RED CAP

Many years ago there lived a dear little girl who was beloved by every one who knew her; but her grand-mother was so very fond of her that she never felt she could think and do enough to please this dear grand-daughter, and she presented the little girl with a red silk cap, which suited her so well, that she would never wear anything else, and so was called Little Red-Cap.

One day Red-Cap's mother said to her, "Come, Red-Cap, here is a nice piece of meat, and a bottle of wine: take these to your grandmother; she is weak and ailing, and they will do her good. Be there before she gets up; go quietly and carefully."

The grandmother lived far away in the wood, a long walk from the village, and as Little Red-Cap came among the trees she met a Wolf; but she did not know what a wicked animal it was, and so she was not at all frightened. "Good morning, Little Red-Cap," he said.

"Thank you, Mr. Wolf," said she.

"Where are you going so early, Little Red-Cap?"

"To my grandmother's," she answered.

"And what are you carrying in that basket?"

"Some wine and meat," she replied. "We baked the meat yesterday, so that grandmother, who is very weak, might have a nice strengthening meal."

"And where does your grandmother live?" asked the Wolf.

"Oh, quite twenty minutes walk further in the forest. The cottage stands under three great oak trees; and close by are some nut bushes, by which you will at once know it."

The Wolf was thinking to himself, "She is a nice tender thing, and will taste better than the old woman; I must act cleverly, that I may make a meal of both."

Presently he came up again to Little Red-Cap, and said, "Just look at the beautiful flowers which grow around you; why do you not look about you? I believe you don't hear how sweetly the birds are singing. You walk as if you were going to school; see how cheerful everything is about you in the forest."

And Little Red-Cap opened her eyes; and when she saw how the sunbeams glanced and danced through the trees, and what bright flowers were blooming in her path, she thought, "If I take my grandmother a fresh nosegay, she will be very much pleased; and it is so very early that I can, even then, get there in good time;" and running into the forest, she looked about for flowers. But when she had once begun she did not know how to leave off, and kept going deeper and deeper amongst the trees looking for some still more beautiful flower. The Wolf, however, ran straight to the house of the old grandmother, and knocked at the door.

"Who's there?" asked the old lady.

"Only Little Red-Cap, bringing you some meat and wine; please open the door," answered the Wolf. "Lift up the latch," cried the grandmother; "I am much too ill to get up myself."

So the Wolf lifted the latch, and the door flew open; and without a word, he jumped on to the bed, and gobbled up the poor old lady. Then he put on her clothes, and tied her night-cap over his head; got into the bed, and drew the blankets over him. All this time Red-Cap was gathering flowers; and when she had picked as many as she could carry, she thought of her grandmother, and hurried to the cottage. She wondered greatly to find the door open; and when she got into the room, she began to feel very ill, and exclaimed, "How sad I feel! I wish I had not come to-day." Then she said, "Good morning," but received no reply; so she went up to the bed, and drew back the curtains, and there lay her grandmother, as she imagined, with the cap drawn half over her eyes, and looking very fierce.

"Oh, grandmother, what great ears you have!" she said.

"All the better to hear you with," was the reply.

"And what great eyes you have!"

"All the better to see you with."

"And what great hands you have!"

"All the better to touch you with."

"But, grandmother, what very great teeth you have!"

"All the better to eat you with;" and hardly were the words spoken when the Wolf made a jump out of bed, and swallowed up poor Little Red-Cap also.

As soon as the Wolf had thus satisfied his hunger, he laid himself down again on the bed, and went to sleep and snored very loudly. A huntsman passing by overheard him, and said, "How loudly that old woman snores! I must see if anything is the matter."

So he went into the cottage; and when he came to the bed, he saw the Wolf sleeping in it. "What! are you here, you old rascal? I have been looking for you," exclaimed he; and taking up his gun, he shot the old Wolf through the head.

But it is also said that the story ends in a different manner; for that one day, when Red-Cap was taking some presents to her grandmother, a Wolf met her, and wanted to mislead her; but she went straight on, and told her grandmother that she had met a Wolf, who said good day, and who looked so hungrily out of his great eyes, as if he would have eaten her up had she not been on the high-road.

So her grandmother said, "We will shut the door, and then he cannot get in." Soon after, up came the Wolf, who tapped, and exclaimed, "I am Little Red-Cap, grandmother; I have some roast meat for you." But they kept quite quiet, and did not open the door; so the Wolf, after looking several times round the house, at last jumped on the roof, thinking to wait till Red-Cap went home in the evening, and then to creep after her and eat her in the darkness. The old woman, however, saw what the villain intended. There stood before the door a large stone trough, and she said to Little Red-Cap, "Take this bucket, dear: yesterday I boiled some meat in this water, now pour it into the stone trough." Then the Wolf sniffed the smell of the meat, and his mouth watered, and he wished very much to taste. At last he stretched his neck too far over, so that he lost his balance, and fell down from the roof, right into the great trough below, and there he was drowned.

# THE GOLDEN GOOSE

There was once a man who had three sons. The youngest was called Dummerly, and was on all occasions scorned and ill-treated by the whole family. It happened that the eldest took it into his head one day to go into the forest to cut wood; and his mother gave him a delicious meat pie and a bottle of wine to take with him, that he might sustain himself at his work. As he went into the forest, a little old man bid him good day, and said, "Give me a little bit of meat from your plate, and a little wine out of your flask; I am very hungry and thirsty." But this clever young man said, "Give you my meat and wine! No, I thank you; there would not be enough left for me;" and he went on his way. He soon began to chop down a tree; but he had not worked long before he missed his stroke, and cut himself, and was obliged to go home and have the wound bound up. Now, it was the little old man who caused him this mischief.

Next the second son went out to work; and his mother gave him, too, a meat pie and a bottle of wine. And the same little old man encountered him also, and begged him for something to eat and drink. But he, too, thought himself extremely clever, and said, "Whatever you get, I shall be without; so go your way!" The little man made sure that he should have his reward; and the second stroke that he struck at a tree, hit him on the leg, so that he too was compelled to go home.

Then Dummerly said, "Father, I should like to go and cut fuel too." But his father replied, "Your brothers have both maimed themselves; you had better stop at home, for you know nothing of the job." But Dummerly was very urgent; and at last his father said, "Go your way; you will be wiser when you have suffered for your foolishness." And his mother gave him only some dry bread, and a bottle of sour ale; but when he went into the forest, he met the little old man, who said, "Give me some meat and drink, for I am very hungry and thirsty." Dummerly said, "I have nothing but dry bread and sour beer; if that will do for you, we will sit down and eat it together." So they sat down, and when the lad took out his bread, behold it was turned into a splendid meat pie, and his sour beer became delicious wine! They ate and drank heartily, and when they had finished, the little man said, "As you have a kind heart, and have been willing to share everything with me I will bring good to you. There stands an old tree; chop it down, and you will find something at the root." Then he took his leave and went his way.

Dummerly set to work, and cut down the tree; and when it fell, he discovered in a hollow under the roots a goose with plumage of pure gold. He took it up, and went on to an inn, where he proposed sleep for the night. The landlord had three daughters, and when they saw the goose, they were very curious to find out what this wonderful bird could be, and wished very much to pluck one of the feathers out of its tail. At last the eldest said, "I must and will have a feather." So she waited till his back was turned, and then caught hold of the goose by the wing; but to her great surprise, there she stuck, for neither hand nor finger could she pull away again. Presently in came the second sister, and thought to have a feather too; but the instant she touched her sister, there she too hung fast. At last came the third, and desired a feather; but the other two cried out, "Keep away! for heaven's sake, keep away!" However, she did not understand what they meant. "If they are there," thought she, "I may as well be there too," so she went up to them. But the moment she touched her sisters she stuck fast, and hung to the goose as they did. And so they abode with the goose all night.

The next morning Dummerly carried off the goose under his arm, and took no heed of the three girls, but went out with them sticking fast behind; and wherever he journeyed, the three were obliged to follow, whether they wished or not, as fast as their legs could carry them.

In the middle of a field the parson met them; and when he saw the procession, he said, "Are you not ashamed of yourselves, you bold girls, to run after the young man like that over the fields? Is that proper behavior?"

Then he took the youngest by the hand to lead her away; but the moment he touched her he, too, hung fast, and followed in the procession.

Presently up came the clerk; and when he saw his master, the parson, running after the three girls, he was greatly surprised, and said, "Hollo! hollo! your reverence! whither so fast! There is a christening to-day."

Then he ran up, and caught him by the gown, and instantly he was fast too.

As the five were thus trudging along, one after another, they met two laborers with their mattocks coming from work; and the parson called out to them to set him free. But hardly had they touched him, when they, too, joined the ranks, and so made seven, all running after Dummerly and his goose.

At last they came to a city, where reigned a King who had an only daughter. The princess was of so thoughtful and serious a turn of mind that no one could make her laugh; and the King had announced to all the world that whoever could make her laugh should have her for his wife. When the young man heard this, he went to her with the goose and all its followers; and as soon as she saw the seven all hanging together, and running about, treading on each other's heels, she could not help bursting into a long and loud laugh.

Then Dummerly claimed her for his bride; the wedding took place, and he was heir to the kingdom, and lived long and happily with his wife.

# BEARSKIN

There was once upon a time a young fellow who enlisted for a soldier, and became so brave and courageous that he was always in the front ranks when it rained blue beans.[1] As long as the war lasted all went well, but when peace was concluded he received his discharge, and the captain told him he might go where he liked. His parents meanwhile had died, and as he had no longer any home to go to he paid a visit to his brothers, and asked them to give him shelter until war broke out again. His brothers, however, were hard-hearted, and said, "What could we do with you? We could make nothing of you; see to what you have brought yourself"; and so turned a deaf ear. The poor Soldier had nothing but his musket left; so he mounted this on his shoulder and set out on a tramp. By and by he came to a great heath with nothing on it but a circle of trees, under which he sat down, sorrowfully considering his fate. "I have no money," thought he; "I have learnt nothing but soldiering, and now, since peace is concluded, there is no need of me. I see well enough I shall have to starve." All at once he heard a rustling, and as he looked round he perceived a stranger standing before him, dressed in a gray coat, who looked very stately, but had an ugly cloven foot. "I know quite well what you need," said this being; "gold and other possessions you shall have, as much as you can spend; but first I must know whether you are a coward or not, that I may not spend my money foolishly."

"A soldier and a coward!" replied the other, "that cannot be; you may put me to any proof."

"Well, then," replied the stranger, "look behind you."

The Soldier turned and saw a huge bear, which eyed him very ferociously. "Oho!" cried he, "I will tickle your nose for you, that you shall no longer be able to grumble"; and, raising his musket, he shot the bear in the forehead, so that he tumbled in a heap upon the ground, and did not stir afterward. Thereupon the stranger said, "I see quite well that you are not wanting in courage; but there is yet one condition which you must fulfil." "If it does not interfere with my future happiness," said the Soldier, who had remarked who it was that addressed him; "if it does not interfere with that, I shall not hesitate."

"That you must see about yourself!" said the stranger. "For the next seven years you must not wash yourself, nor comb your hair or beard, neither must you cut your nails nor say one paternoster. Then I will give you this coat and mantle, which you must wear during these seven years; and if you die within that time you are mine, but if you live you are rich, and free all your life long."

---

[Footnote [1]: Small shot.]

The Soldier reflected for awhile on his great necessities, and, remembering how often he had braved death, he at length consented, and ventured to accept the offer. Thereupon the Evil One pulled off the gray coat, handed it to the soldier, and said, "If you at any time search in the pockets of your coat when you have it on, you will always find your hand full of money." Then also he pulled off the skin of the bear, and said, "That shall be your cloak and your bed; you must sleep on it, and not dare to lie in any other bed, and on this account you shall be called 'Bearskin.'" Immediately the Evil One disappeared.

The Soldier now put on the coat, and dipped his hands into the pockets, to assure himself of the reality of the transaction. Then he hung the bearskin around himself, and went about the world chuckling at his good luck, and buying whatever suited his fancy which money could purchase. For the first year his appearance was not very remarkable, but in the second he began to look quite a monster. His hair covered almost all his face, his beard appeared like a piece of dirty cloth, his nails were claws, and his countenance was so covered with dirt that one might have grown cresses upon it if one had sown seed! Whoever looked at him ran away; but because he gave the poor in every place gold coin they prayed that he might not die during the seven years; and because he paid liberally everywhere, he found a night's lodging without difficulty. In the fourth year he came to an inn where the landlord would not take him in, and refused even to give him a place in his stables, lest the horses should be frightened and become restive. However, when Bearskin put his hand into his pocket and drew it out full of gold ducats the landlord yielded the point, and gave him a place in the outbuildings, but not till he had promised that he would not show himself, for fear the inn should gain a bad name.

While Bearskin sat by himself in the evening, wishing from his heart that the seven years were over, he heard in the corner a loud groan. Now the old Soldier had a compassionate heart, so he opened the door and saw an old man weeping violently and wringing his hands. Bearskin stepped nearer, but the old man jumped up and tried to escape; but when he recognized a human voice he let himself be persuaded, and by kind words and soothings on the part of the old Soldier he at length disclosed the cause of his distress. His property had dwindled away by degrees, and he and his daughters would have to starve, for he was so poor that he had not the money to pay the host, and would therefore be put into prison.

"If you have no care except that," replied Bearskin, "I have money enough"; and causing the landlord to be called, he paid him, and put a purse full of gold besides into the pocket of the old man. The latter, when he saw himself released from his troubles, knew not how to be sufficiently grateful, and said to the Soldier, "Come with me; my daughters are all wonders of beauty, so choose one of them for a wife. When they hear what you have done for me they will not refuse you. You appear certainly an uncommon man, but they will soon put you to rights."

This speech pleased Bearskin, and he went with the old man. As soon as the eldest daughter saw him, she was so terrified at his countenance that she shrieked out and ran away. The second one stopped and looked at him from head to foot; but at last she said, "How can I take a husband who has not a bit of a human countenance? The grizzly bear would have pleased me better who came to see us once, and gave himself out as a man, for he wore a hussar's hat, and had white gloves on besides."

But the youngest daughter said, "Dear father, this must be a good man who has assisted you out of your troubles; if you have promised him a bride for the service your word must be kept"

It was a pity the man's face was covered with dirt and hair, else one would have seen how glad at heart these words made him. Bearskin took a ring off his finger, broke it in two, and, giving the youngest daughter one half, he kept the other for himself. On her half he wrote his name, and on his own he wrote hers, and begged her to preserve it carefully. Thereupon he took leave, saying, "For three years longer I must wander about; if I come back again, then we will celebrate our wedding; but if I do not, you are free, for I shall be dead. But pray to God that he will preserve my life."

When he was gone the poor bride clothed herself in black, and whenever she thought of her bridegroom burst into tears. From her sisters she received nothing but scorn and mocking. "Pay great attention when he shakes your hand," said the eldest, "and you will see his beautiful claws!" "Take care!" said the second, "bears are fond of sweets, and if you please him he will eat you up, perhaps!" "You must mind and do his will," continued the eldest, "or he will begin growling!" And the second daughter said further, "But the wedding will certainly be merry, for bears dance well!" The bride kept silence, and would not be drawn from her purpose by all these taunts; and meanwhile Bearskin wandered about in the world, doing good where he could, and giving liberally to the poor, for which they prayed heartily for him. At length the last day of the seven years approached, and Bearskin went and sat down again on the heath beneath the circle of trees. In a very short time the wind whistled, and the Evil One presently stood before him and looked at him with a vexed face. He threw the Soldier his old coat and demanded his gray one back. "We have not got so far as that yet," replied Bearskin; "you must clean me first." Then the Evil One had, whether he liked it or no, to fetch water, wash the old Soldier, comb his hair out, and cut his nails. This done, he appeared again like a brave warrior, and indeed was much handsomer than before.

As soon as the Evil One had disappeared, Bearskin became quite light-hearted; and going into the nearest town he bought a fine velvet coat, and hired a carriage drawn by four white horses, in which he was driven to the house of his bride. Nobody knew him; the father took him for some celebrated general, and led him into the room where his daughters were. He was compelled to sit down between the two eldest, and they offered him wine, and heaped his plate with the choicest morsels; for they thought they had never seen any one so handsome before. But the bride sat opposite to him dressed in black, neither opening her eyes nor speaking a word. At length the Soldier asked the father if he would give him one of his daughters to wife, and immediately the two elder sisters arose, and ran to their chambers to dress themselves out in their most becoming clothes, for each thought she should be chosen. Meanwhile the stranger, as soon as he found himself alone with his bride, pulled out the half of the ring and threw it into a cup of wine, which he handed across the table. She took it, and as soon as she had drunk it and seen the half ring lying at the bottom her heart beat rapidly, and she produced the other half, which she wore round her neck on a riband. She held them together, and they joined each other exactly, and the stranger said, "I am your bridegroom, whom you first saw as Bearskin; but through God's mercy I have regained my human form, and am myself once more." With these words he embraced and kissed her; and at the same time the two eldest sisters entered in full costume. As soon as they saw that the very handsome man had fallen to the share of their youngest sister, and heard that he was the same as "Bearskin," they ran out of the house full of rage and jealousy.

# CINDERELLA

The wife of a rich man fell sick: and when she felt that her end drew nigh, she called her only daughter to her bedside, and said, "Always be a good girl, and I will look down from heaven and watch over you." Soon afterwards she shut her eyes and died, and was buried in the garden; and the little girl went every day to her grave and wept, and was always good and kind to all about her. And the snow spread a beautiful white covering over the grave; but by the time the sun had melted it away again, her father had married another wife. This new wife had two daughters of her own: they were fair in face but foul at heart, and it was now a sorry time for the poor little girl. "What does the good-for-nothing thing want in the parlor?" said they; and they took away her fine clothes, and gave her an old frock to put on, and laughed at her and turned her into the kitchen.

Then she was forced to do hard work; to rise early, before daylight, to bring the water, to make the fire, to cook and to wash. She had no bed to lie down on, but was made to lie by the hearth among the ashes, and they called her Cinderella.

It happened once that her father was going to the fair, and asked his wife's daughters what he should bring to them. "Fine clothes," said the first. "Pearls and diamonds," said the second. "Now, child," said he to his own daughter, "what will you have?" "The first sprig, dear father, that rubs against your hat on your way home," said she. Then he bought for the two first the fine clothes and pearls and diamonds they had asked for: and on his way home, as he rode through a green copse, a sprig of hazel brushed against him, so he broke it off and when he got home he gave it to his daughter. Then she took it, and went to her mother's grave and planted it there, and cried so much that it was watered with her tears; and there it grew and became a fine tree, and soon a little bird came and built its nest upon the tree, and talked with her and watched over her, and brought her whatever she wished for.

Now it happened that the king of the land held a feast which was to last three days, and out of those who came to it his son was to choose a bride for himself; and Cinderella's two sisters were asked to come. So they called Cinderella, and said, "Now, comb our hair, brush our shoes, and tie our sashes for us, for we are going to dance at the king's feast." Then she did as she was told, but when all was done she could not help crying, for she thought to herself, she would have liked to go to the dance too, and at last she begged her mother very hard to let her go, "You! Cinderella?" said she; "you who have nothing to wear, no clothes at all, and who cannot even dance—you want to go to the ball?" And when she kept on begging, to get rid of her, she said at last, "I will throw this basinful of peas into the ash heap, and if you have picked them all out in two hours' time you shall go to the feast too." Then she threw the peas into the ashes; but the little maiden ran out at the back door into the garden, and cried out—

"Hither, thither, through the sky, turtle-doves and linnets, fly!
Blackbird, thrush, and chaffinch gay, hither, thither, haste away!
One and all, come, help me quick! haste ye, haste ye—pick, pick, pick!"

Then first came two white doves; and next two turtle-doves; and after them all the little birds under heaven came, and the little doves stooped their heads down and set to work, pick, pick, pick; and then the others began to pick, pick, pick, and picked out all the good grain and put it into a dish, and left the ashes. At the end of one hour the work was done, and all flew out again at the windows. Then she brought the dish to her mother. But the mother said, "No, no! indeed, you have no clothes and cannot dance; you shall not go." And when Cinderella begged very hard to go, she said, "If you can in one hour's time pick two of these dishes of pease out of the ashes, you shall go too." So she shook two dishes of peas into the ashes; but the little maiden went out into the garden at the back of the house, and called as before and all the birds came flying, and in half an hour's time all was done, and out they flew again. And then Cinderella took the dishes to her mother, rejoicing to think that she should now go to the ball. But her mother said, "It is all of no use, you cannot go; you have no clothes, and cannot dance; and you would only put us to shame;" and off she went with her two daughters to the feast.

Now when all were gone, and nobody left at home, Cinderella went sorrowfully and sat down under the hazel-tree, and cried out—

"Shake, shake, hazel-tree, gold and silver over me!"

Then her friend the bird flew out of the tree and brought a gold and silver dress for her, and slippers of spangled silk; and she put them on, and followed her sisters to the feast. But they did not know her, she looked so fine and beautiful in her rich clothes.

The king's son soon came up to her, and took her by the hand and danced with her and no one else; and he never left her hand, but when any one else came to ask her to dance, he said, "This lady is dancing with me." Thus they danced till a late hour of the night, and then

she wanted to go home; and the king's son said, "I shall go and take care of you to your home," for he wanted to see where the beautiful maid lived. But she slipped away from him unawares, and ran off towards home, and the prince followed her; then she jumped up into the pigeon-house and shut the door. So he waited till her father came home, and told him that the unknown maiden who had been at the feast had hidden herself in the pigeon-house. But when they had broken open the door they found no one within; and as they came back into the house, Cinderella lay, as she always did, in her dirty frock by the ashes; for she had run as quickly as she could through the pigeon-house and on to the hazel-tree, and had there taken off her beautiful clothes, and laid them beneath the tree, that the bird might carry them away; and had seated herself amid the ashes again in her little old frock.

The next day, when the feast was again held, and her father, mother and sisters were gone, Cinderella went to the hazel-tree, and all happened as the evening before.

The king's son, who was waiting for her, took her by the hand and danced with her; and, when any one asked her to dance, he said as before, "This lady is dancing with me." When night came she wanted to go home; and the king's son went with her, but she sprang away from him all at once into the garden behind her father's house. In this garden stood a fine large pear-tree; and Cinderella jumped up into it without being seen. Then the king's son waited till her father came home, and said to him, "The unknown lady has slipped away, and I think she must have sprung into the pear-tree." The father ordered an axe to be brought, and they cut down the tree, but found no one upon it. And when they came back into the kitchen, there lay Cinderella in the ashes as usual; for she had slipped down on the other side of the tree, and carried her beautiful clothes back to the bird at the hazel-tree, and then put on her little old frock.

The third day, when her father and mother and sisters were gone, she went again into the garden, and said—

"Shake, shake, hazel-tree, gold and silver over me!"

Then her kind friend the bird brought a dress still finer than the former one, and slippers which were all of gold; and the king's son danced with her alone, and when any one else asked her to dance, he said, "This lady is my partner." Now when night came she wanted to go home; and the king's son would go with her, but she managed to slip away from him, though in such a hurry that she dropped her left golden slipper upon the stairs.

So the prince took the shoe, and went the next day to the king, his father, and said, "I will take for my wife the lady that this golden shoe fits."

Then both the sisters were overjoyed to hear this; for they had beautiful feet, and had no doubt that they could wear the golden slipper. The eldest went first into the room where the slipper was, and wanted to try it on, and the mother stood by. But her big toe could not go into it, and the shoe was altogether much too small for her. Then the mother said, "Never mind, cut it off. When you are queen you will not care about toes; you will not want to go on foot." So the silly girl cut her big toe off, and squeezed the shoe on, and went to the king's son. Then he took her for his bride, and rode away with her.

But on their way home they had to pass by the hazel-tree that Cinderella had planted, and there sat a little dove on the branch, singing—

"Back again! back again! look to the shoe!
The shoe is too small, and not made for you!
Prince! prince! look again for thy bride,
For she's not the true one that sits by thy side."

Then the prince looked at her foot, and saw by the blood that streamed from it what a trick she had played him. So he brought the false bride back to her home, and said, "This is not the right bride; let the other sister try and put on the slipper." Then she went into the room and got her foot into the shoe, all but the heel, which was too large. But her mother squeezed it in till the blood came, and took her to the king's son; and he rode away with her. But when they came to the hazel-tree, the little dove sat there still, and sang as before. Then the king's son looked down, and saw that the blood streamed from the shoe. So he brought her back again also. "This is not the true bride," said he to the father; "have you no other daughters?"

Then Cinderella came and she took her clumsy shoe off, and put on the golden slipper, and it fitted as if it had been made for her. And when he drew near and looked at her face the prince knew her, and said, "This is the right bride."

Then he took Cinderella on his horse and rode away. And when they came to the hazel-tree the white dove sang—

"Prince! prince! take home thy bride,
For she is the true one that sits by thy side!"

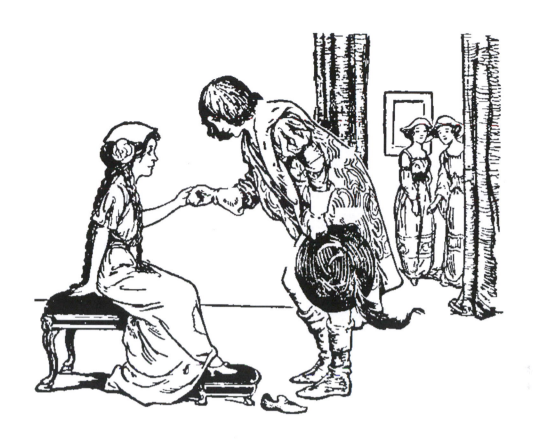

# FAITHFUL JOHN

Once upon a time there lived an old King, who fell very sick, and thought he was lying upon his death-bed; so he said, "Let faithful John come to me." This faithful John was his affectionate servant, and was so called because he had been true to him all his lifetime. As soon as John came to the bedside, the King said, "My faithful John, I feel that my end approaches, and I have no other care than about my son, who is still so young that he cannot always guide himself aright. If you do not promise to instruct him in everything he ought to know, and to be his guardian, I cannot close my eyes in peace." Then John answered, "I will never leave him; I will always serve him truly, even if it costs me my life." So the old King was comforted, and said, "Now I can die in peace. After my death you must show him all the chambers, halls, and vaults in the castle, and all the treasures which are in them; but the last room in the long corridor you must not show him, for in it hangs the portrait of the daughter of the King of the Golden Palace; if he sees her picture, he will conceive a great love for her, and will fall down in a swoon, and on her account undergo great perils, therefore you must keep him away." The faithful John pressed his master's hand again in token of assent, and soon after the King laid his head upon the pillow and expired.

After the old King had been borne to his grave, the faithful John related to the young King all that his father had said upon his death-bed, and declared, "All this I will certainly fulfil; I will be as true to you as I was to him, if it costs me my life." When the time of mourning was passed, John said to the young King, "It is now time for you to see your inheritance; I will show you your paternal castle." So he led the King all over it, upstairs and downstairs, and showed him all the riches, and all the splendid chambers; only one room he did not open, containing the perilous portrait, which was so placed that one saw it directly the door was opened, and, moreover, it was so beautifully painted that one thought it breathed and moved; nothing in all the world could be more lifelike or more beautiful. The young King remarked, however, that the faithful John always passed by one door, so he asked, "Why do you not open that one?" "There is something in it," he replied, "which will frighten you."

But the King said, "I have seen all the rest of the castle, and I will know what is in there," and he went and tried to open the door by force. The faithful John pulled him back, and said, "I promised your father before he died that you should not see the contents of that room; it would bring great misfortunes both upon you and me."

"Oh, no," replied the young King, "if I do not go in it will be my certain ruin; I should have no peace night nor day until I had seen it with my own eyes. Now I will not stir from the place till you unlock the door."

Then the faithful John saw that it was of no use talking; so, with a heavy heart and many sighs, he picked the key out of the great bunch. When he had opened the door, he went in first, and thought he would cover up the picture, that the King should not see it; but it was of no use, for the King stepped upon tiptoes and looked over his shoulder; and as soon as he saw the portrait of the maiden, which was so beautiful and glittered with precious stones, he fell down on the ground insensible. The faithful John lifted him up and carried him to his bed, and thought with great concern, "Mercy on us! the misfortune has happened; what will come of it?" and he gave the young King wine until he came to himself. The first words he spoke were, "Who does that beautiful picture represent?" "That is the daughter of the King of the Golden Palace," was the reply.

"Then," said the King, "my love for her is so great that if all the leaves on the trees had tongues, they should not gainsay it; my life is set upon the search for her. You are my faithful John, you must accompany me."

The trusty servant deliberated for a long while how to set about this business, for it was very difficult to get into the presence of the King's daughter. At last he bethought himself of a way, and said to the King, "Everything which she has around her is of gold—chairs, tables, dishes, bowls, and all the household utensils. Among your treasures are five tons of gold; let one of the goldsmiths of your kingdom manufacture vessels and utensils of all kinds therefrom—all kinds of birds, and wild and wonderful beasts, such as will please her, then we will travel with these, and try our luck." Then the King summoned all his goldsmiths, who worked day and night until many very beautiful things were ready. When all had been placed on board a ship, the faithful John put on merchant's clothes, and the King likewise, so that they might travel quite unknown. Then they sailed over the wide sea, and sailed away until they came to the city where dwelt the daughter of the King of the Golden Palace.

The faithful John told the King to remain in the ship, and wait for him. "Perhaps," said he, "I shall bring the King's daughter with me; therefore take care that all is in order, and set out the golden vessels and adorn the whole ship." Thereupon John placed in a napkin some of the golden cups, stepped upon land, and went straight to the King's palace. When he came into the castle yard, a beautiful maid stood by the brook, who had two golden pails in her hand, drawing water; and when she had filled them and had turned round, she saw a strange man, and asked who he was. Then John answered, "I am a merchant"; and opening his napkin he showed her its contents. Then she exclaimed, "Oh, what beautiful golden things!" and, setting the pails down, she looked at the cups one after another, and said, "The King's daughter must see these; she is so pleased with anything made of gold that she will buy all these." And taking him by the hand, she led him in; for she was the lady's maid. When the King's daughter saw the golden cups, she was much pleased, and said, "They are so finely worked that I will purchase them all." But the faithful John replied, "I am only the servant of a rich merchant; what I have here is nothing in comparison to those which my master has in his ship, than which nothing more delicate or costly has ever been worked in gold." Then the King's daughter wished to have them all brought; but he said, "It would take many days, and so great is the quantity that your palace has not halls enough in it to place them around." Then her curiosity and desire were still more excited, and at last she said, "Take me to the ship; I will go myself and look at your master's treasure."

The faithful John conducted her to the ship with great joy, and the King, when he beheld her, saw that her beauty was still greater than the picture had represented, and thought nothing else but that his heart would jump out of his mouth. Presently she stepped on board, and the King conducted her below; but the faithful John remained on deck by the steersman, and told him to unmoor the ship and put on all the sail he could, that it might fly as a bird through the air. Meanwhile the King showed the Princess all the golden treasures—the dishes, cups, bowls, the birds, the wild and wonderful beasts. Many hours passed away while she looked at everything, and in her joy she did not remark that the ship sailed on and on. As soon as she had looked at the last, and thanked the merchant, she wished to depart. But when she came on deck, she perceived that they were upon the high sea, far from the shore, and were hastening on with all sail. "Ah," she exclaimed in affright, "I am betrayed; I am carried off and taken away in the power of a strange merchant. I would rather die!"

But the King, taking her by the hand, said, "I am not a merchant, but a king, thine equal in birth. It is true that I have carried thee off; but that is because of my overwhelming love for thee. Dost thou know that when I first saw the portrait of thy beauteous face I fell down in a swoon before it?" When the King's daughter heard these words, she was reassured, and her heart was inclined toward him, so that she willingly became his bride. While they thus went on their voyage on the high sea, it happened that the faithful John, as he sat on the deck of the ship, playing music, saw three crows in the air, who came flying toward them. He stopped playing, and listened to what they were saying to each other, for he understood them perfectly. The first one exclaimed, "There he is, carrying home the daughter of the King of the Golden Palace." "But he is not home yet," replied the second. "But he has her," said the third; "she is sitting by him in the ship." Then the first began again, and exclaimed,

"What matters that? When they go on shore a fox-colored horse will spring toward them, on which he will mount; and as soon as he is on it, it will jump up with him into the air, so that he will never again see his bride." The second one asked, "Is there no escape?" "Oh, yes, if another mounts behind quickly, and takes out the firearms which are in the holster, and with them shoots the horse dead, then the young King will be saved. But who knows that? And if any one does know it, and tells him, such a one will be turned to stone from the toe to the knee." Then the second spoke again, "I know still more: if the horse should be killed, the young King will not then retain his bride; for when they come into the castle a beautiful bridal shirt will lie there upon a dish, and seem to be woven of gold and silver, but it is nothing but sulphur and pitch, and if he puts it on it will burn him to his marrow and bones." Then the third Crow asked, "Is there no escape?" "Oh, yes," answered the second, "if some one takes up the shirt with his glove on, and throws it into the fire, so that it is burnt, the young King will be saved. But what does that signify? Whoever knows it, and tells him, will be turned to stone from his knee to his heart." Then the third Crow spoke: "I know still more: even if the bridal shirt be consumed, still the young King will not retain his bride. For if, after the wedding, a dance is held, while the young Queen dances she will suddenly turn pale, and fall down as if dead; and if some one does not raise her up, and take three drops of blood from her right breast and throw them away, she will die. But whoever knows that, and tells it, will have his whole body turned to stone, from the crown of his head to the toes of his feet."

After the crows had thus talked with one another, they flew away, and the trusty John, who had perfectly understood all they had said, was from that time very quiet and sad; for if he concealed from his master what he had heard, misfortune would happen to him, and if he told him all he must give up his own life. But at last he thought, "I will save my master, even if I destroy myself."

As soon as they came on shore, it happened just as the Crow had foretold, and an immense fox-red horse sprang up. "Capital!" said the King, "this shall carry me to my castle," and he tried to mount; but the faithful John came straight up, and swinging himself quickly on, drew the firearms out of the holster and shot the horse dead. Then the other servants of the King, who were not on good terms with the faithful John, exclaimed, "How shameful to kill the beautiful creature, which might have borne the King to the castle!" But the King replied, "Be silent, and let him go; he is my very faithful John—who knows the good he may have done?" Now they went into the castle, and there stood a dish in the hall, and the splendid bridal shirt lay in it, and seemed nothing else than gold and silver. The young King went up to it and wished to take it up, but the faithful John pushed him away, and taking it up with his gloves on, bore it quickly to the fire and let it burn. The other servants thereupon began to murmur, saying, "See, now he is burning the King's bridal shirt!" But the young King replied, "Who knows what good he has done? Let him alone—he is my faithful John."

Soon after, the wedding was celebrated, and a grand ball was given, and the bride began to dance. So the faithful John paid great attention, and watched her countenance; all at once she grew pale, and fell as if dead to the ground. Then he sprang up hastily, raised her up and bore her to a chamber, where he laid her down, kneeled beside her, and drawing the three drops of blood out of her right breast, threw them away. As soon as she breathed again, she raised herself up; but the young King had witnessed everything, and not knowing why the faithful John had done this was very angry, and called out, "Throw him into prison!" The next morning the trusty John was brought up for trial, and led to the gallows; and as he stood upon them, and was about to be executed, he said, "Every one condemned to die may once before his death speak. Shall I also have that privilege?" "Yes," answered the King, "it shall be granted you." Then the faithful John replied, "I have been unrighteously judged, and have always been true to you"; and he narrated the conversation of the crows which he heard at sea; and how, in order to save his master, he was obliged to do all he had done. Then the King cried out, "Oh, my most trusty John, pardon, pardon; lead him away!" But the trusty John had fallen down at the last word and was turned into stone.

At this event both the King and the Queen were in great grief, and the King thought, "Ah, how wickedly have I rewarded his great fidelity!" and he had the stone statue raised up and placed in his sleeping-chamber, near his bed; and as often as he looked at it, he wept and said, "Ah, could I bring you back to life again, my faithful John!"

After some time had passed, the Queen bore twins, two little sons, who were her great joy. Once, when the Queen was in church, and the two children at home playing by their father's side, he looked up at the stone statue full of sorrow, and exclaimed with a sigh, "Ah, could I restore you to life, my faithful John!" At these words the statue began to speak, saying, "Yes, you can make me alive again, if you will bestow on me that which is dearest to you." The

King replied, "All that I have in the world I will give up for you." The statue spake again: "If you, with your own hand, cut off the heads of both your children, and sprinkle me with their blood, I shall be brought to life again." The King was terrified when he heard that he must himself kill his two dear children; but he remembered his servant's great fidelity, and how the faithful John had died for him, and drawing his sword he cut off the heads of both his children with his own hand. And as soon as he had sprinkled the statue with blood, life came back to it, and the trusty John stood again alive and well before him, and said, "Your faith shall not go unrewarded"; and taking the heads of the two children he set them on again, and anointed their wounds with their blood, and thereupon they healed again in a moment, and the children sprang away and played as if nothing had happened.

Now the King was full of happiness, and as soon as he saw the Queen coming, he hid the faithful John and both the children in a great closet. As soon as she came in he said to her, "Have you prayed in the church?" "Yes," she answered; "but I thought continually of the faithful John, who has come to such misfortune through us." Then he replied, "My dear wife, we can restore his life again to him, but it will cost us both our little sons, whom we must sacrifice." The Queen became pale and was terrified at heart, but she said, "We are guilty of his life on account of his great fidelity." Then he was very glad that she thought as he did, and going up to the closet, he unlocked it, brought out the children and the faithful John, saying, "God be praised! he is saved, and we have still our little sons"; and then he told her all that happened. Afterward they lived happily together to the end of their days.

# THE WATER OF LIFE

Once upon a time there was a King who was so ill that everybody despaired of his life, and his three sons were very sorry, and went out into the palace gardens to weep. There they met an old man, who asked the cause of their grief, and they told him their Father was so ill that he must die, for nothing could save him. The old Man said, "I know a means of saving him: if he drinks of the water of life it will restore him to health; but it is very difficult to find."

"I will soon find it," said the eldest Son, and, going to the sick King, he begged his permission to set out in search of the water of life, which alone could save him. "No; the danger is too great," said the King; "I prefer to die." Nevertheless, the Son begged and entreated so long that the King consented, and the Prince went away, thinking in his own heart, "If I bring this water I am the dearest to my Father, and I shall inherit his kingdom."

After he had ridden a long way he met a Dwarf on the road, who asked him, "Whither away so quickly?"

"You stupid dandyprat," replied the Prince proudly, "why should I tell you that?" and he rode off. But the little Man was angry and he wished an evil thing, so that, soon after, the Prince came into a narrow mountain-pass, and the farther he rode the narrower it grew, till at last it was so close that he could get no farther; but neither could he turn his horse round, nor dismount, and he sat there like one amazed. Meanwhile the sick King waited a long while for him, but he did not come; and the second Son asked leave to go too and seek the water, for he thought to himself, "If my Brother is dead the kingdom comes to me." At first the King refused to spare him, but he gave way, and the Prince set out on the same road as the elder one had taken, and met also the same Dwarf, who stopped him and asked him, "Whither ride you so hastily?" "Little dandyprat," replied the Prince, "what do you want to know for?" and he rode off without looking round. The Dwarf, however, enchanted him, and it happened to him as it had to his Brother: he came to a defile where he could move neither forward nor backward. Such is the fate of all haughty people.

Now, when the second Son did not return, the youngest begged leave to go and fetch the water, and the King was obliged at last to give his consent. When he met the Dwarf, and was asked whither he was going so hurriedly, he stopped and replied, "I seek the water of life, for my Father is sick unto death." "Do you know where to find it?" asked the Dwarf. "No," replied the Prince. "Since you have behaved yourself as you ought," said the Dwarf, "and not haughtily like your false Brothers, I will give you information and show you where you may obtain the water of life. It flows from a fountain in the court of an enchanted castle, into which you can never penetrate if I do not give you an iron rod and two loaves of bread. With the rod knock thrice at the iron door of the castle, and it will spring open. Within lie two lions with open jaws, but if you throw down to each a loaf of bread they will be quiet. Then hasten and fetch some of the water of life before it strikes twelve, for then the door will shut again, and you will be imprisoned."

The Prince thanked the Dwarf, and, taking the rod and bread, he set out on his journey, and as he arrived at the castle he found it as the Dwarf had said. At the third knock the door sprang open; and, when he had stilled the lions with the bread, he walked into a fine, large hall, where sat several enchanted Princes, from whose fingers he drew off the rings, and he also took away with him a sword and some bread which lay there. A little farther on he came to a room wherein stood a beautiful maiden, who was so pleased to see him that she kissed him and said he had freed her, and should have her whole kingdom, and if he came in another year their wedding should be celebrated. Then she told him where the fountain of water of life was placed, and he hastened away lest it should strike twelve ere he gained it. He came next into a room where a fine, clean covered bed stood, and, being tired, he lay down to rest himself a bit. But he went to sleep, and when he awoke it struck the quarter to twelve, and the sound made him hurry to the fountain, from which he took some water in a cup which stood near. This done, he hastened to the door, and was scarcely out before it struck twelve, and the door swung to so heavily that it carried away a piece of his heel.

But he was very glad, in spite of this, that he had procured the water, and he journeyed homeward, and passed again where the Dwarf stood. When the Dwarf saw the sword and bread which he had brought away he declared he had done well, for with the sword he could destroy whole armies—but the bread was worth nothing. Now, the Prince was not willing to return home to his Father without his Brothers, and so he said to the Dwarf, "Dear Dwarf, can you tell me where my Brothers are? They went out before me in search of the water of life, and did not return." "They are stuck fast between two mountains," replied the Dwarf; "because they were so haughty, I enchanted them there."

Then the Prince begged for their release, till at last the Dwarf brought them out; but he warned the youngest to beware of them, for they had evil in their hearts.

When his Brothers came he was very glad, and he related to them all that had happened to him; how he had found the water of life and brought away a cupful of it; and how he had rescued a beautiful Princess, who for a whole year was going to wait for him, and then he was to return to be married to her, and receive a rich kingdom. After this tale the three Brothers rode away together, and soon entered a province where there were war and famine raging, and the King thought he should perish, so great was his necessity. The youngest Prince went to this King and gave him the bread, with which he fed and satisfied his whole people; and then the Prince gave him the sword, wherewith he defeated and slew all his enemies, and regained peace and quiet. This effected, the Prince took back the bread and sword, and rode on farther with his Brothers, and by and by they came to two other provinces where also war and famine were destroying the people. To each King the Prince lent his bread and sword, and so saved three kingdoms. After, this they went on board a ship to pass over the sea which separated them from home, and during the voyage the two elder Brothers said to one another, "Our Brother has found the water of life and we have not; therefore our Father will give the kingdom which belongs to us to him, and our fortune will be taken away." Indulging these thoughts they became so envious that they consulted together how they should kill him, and one day, waiting till he was fast asleep, they poured the water out of his cup and took it for themselves, while they filled his up with bitter salt water. As soon as they arrived at home the youngest Brother took his cup to the sick King, that he might drink out of it and regain his health. But scarcely had he drunk a very little of the water when he became worse than before, for it was as bitter as wormwood. While the King lay in this state, the two elder Princes came, and accused their Brother of poisoning their Father; but they had brought the right water, and they handed it to the King. Scarcely had he drunk a little out of the cup when the King felt his sickness leave him, and soon he was as strong and healthy as in his young days. The two Brothers now went to the youngest Prince, mocking him, and saying, "You certainly found the water of life; but you had the trouble and we had the reward; you should have been more cautious and kept your eyes open, for we took your cup while you were asleep on the sea; and, moreover, in a year one of us intends to fetch your Princess. Beware, however, that you betray us not; the King will not believe you, and if you say a single word your life will be lost; but if you remain silent you are safe." The old King, nevertheless, was very angry with his youngest Son, who had conspired, as he believed, against his life. He caused his court to be assembled, and sentence was given to the effect that the Prince should be secretly shot; and once as he rode out hunting, unsuspicious of any evil, the Huntsman was sent with him to perform the deed. By and by, when they were alone in the wood, the Huntsman seemed so sad that the Prince asked him what ailed him. The Huntsman replied, "I cannot and yet must tell you." "Tell me boldly what it is," said the Prince, "I will forgive you." "Ah, it is no other than that I must shoot you, for so has the King ordered me," said the Huntsman, with a deep sigh.

The Prince was frightened, and said, "Let me live, dear Huntsman, let me live! I will give you my royal coat and you shall give me yours in exchange." To this the Huntsman readily assented, for he felt unable to shoot the Prince, and after they had exchanged their clothing the Huntsman returned home, and the Prince went deeper into the wood.

A short time afterward three wagons laden with gold and precious stones came to the King's palace for his youngest Son. They were sent by the three Kings in token of gratitude for the sword which had defeated their enemies, and the bread which had nourished their people. At this arrival the old King said to himself, "Perhaps, after all, my Son was guiltless," and he lamented to his courtiers that he had let his Son be killed. But the Huntsman cried out, "He lives yet! for I could not find it in my heart to fulfil your commands"; and he told the King how it had happened. The King felt as if a stone had been removed from his heart, and he caused it to be proclaimed everywhere throughout his dominions that his Son might return and would again be taken into favor.

Meanwhile the Princess had caused a road to be made up to her castle of pure shining gold, and she told her attendants that whoever should ride straight up this road would be the right person, and one whom they might admit into the castle; but, on the contrary, whoever should ride up not on the road, but by the side, they were ordered on no account to admit, for he was not the right person. When, therefore, the time came round which the Princess had mentioned to the youngest Prince, the eldest Brother thought he would hasten to her castle and announce himself as her deliverer, that he might gain her as a bride and the kingdom besides. So he rode away, and when he came in front of the castle and saw the fine golden road he thought it would be a shame to ride thereon, and so he turned to the left hand and rode up out of the road. But as he came up to the door the guards told him he was not the right person, and he must ride back again. Soon afterward the second Prince also set out, and he, likewise, when he came to the golden road and his horse set its forefeet upon it, thought it would be a pity to travel upon it, so he turned aside to the right hand and went up. When he came to the gate the guards refused him admittance, and told him he was not the person expected, and so he had to return homeward. The youngest Prince, who had all this time been wandering about in the forest, had also remembered that the year was up, and soon after his Brothers' departure he appeared before the castle and rode up straight on the golden road, for he was so deeply engaged in thinking of his beloved Princess that he did not observe it. As soon as he arrived at the door it was opened, and the Princess received him with joy, saving he was her deliverer and the lord of her dominions. Soon after their wedding was celebrated, and when it was over the Princess told her husband that his Father had forgiven him and desired to see him. Thereupon he rode to the old King's palace, and told him how his Brothers had betrayed him while he slept, and had sworn him to silence. When the King heard this he would have punished the false Brothers, but they had prudently taken themselves off in a ship, and they never returned home afterward.

# THUMBLING

There was once a poor peasant who sat in the evening by the hearth and poked the fire, and his wife sat and span. Then said he, "How sad it is that we have no children! With us all is so quiet, and in other houses it is noisy and lively."

"Yes," replied the wife, and sighed, "even if we had only one, and it were quite small, and only as big as a thumb, I should be quite satisfied, and we would still love it with all our hearts." Now it so happened that their wish was granted and a child was given them, but although it was perfect in all its limbs, it was no longer than a thumb. Then said they, "It is as we wished it to be, and it shall be our dear child;" and because of its size, they called it Thumbling. They did not let it want for food, but the child did not grow taller, but remained as it had been at the first, nevertheless it looked sensibly out of its eyes, and soon showed itself to be a wise and nimble creature, for everything it did turned out well.

One day the peasant was getting ready to go into the forest to cut wood, when he said as if to himself, "How I wish that there was any one who would bring the cart to me!" "Oh, father," cried Thumbling, "I will soon bring the cart; rely on that; it shall be in the forest at the appointed time." The man smiled and said, "How can that be done; you are far too small to lead the horse by the reins?" "That's of no consequence, father, if my mother will only harness it, I will sit in the horse's ear, and call out to him how he is to go." "Well," answered the man, "for once we will try it."

When the time came, the mother harnessed the horse, and placed Thumbling in its ear, and then the little creature cried, "Gee up, gee up!"

Then it went quite properly as if with its master, and the cart went the right way into the forest. It so happened that just as he was turning a corner, and the little one was crying, "Gee up," two strange men came towards him. "My word!" said one of them. "What is this? There is a cart coming, and a driver is calling to the horse, and still he is not to be seen!" "That can't be right," said the other, "we will follow the cart and see where it stops." The cart, however, drove right into the forest, and exactly to the place where the wood had been cut. When Thumbling saw his father, he cried to him, "See, father, here I am with the cart; now take me down." The father got hold of the horse with his left hand, and with the right took his little son out of the ear. Thumbling sat down quite merrily on a straw, but when the two strange men saw him, they did not know what to say for astonishment. Then one of them took the other aside and said, "Hark, the little fellow would make our fortune if we exhibited him in a large town, for money. We will buy him." They went to the peasant and said, "Sell us the little man. He shall be well treated with us." "No," replied the father, "he is the apple of my eye, and all the money in the world cannot buy him from me." Thumbling, however, when he heard of the bargain, had crept up the folds of his father's coat, placed himself on his shoulder, and whispered in his ear. "Father, do give me away; I will soon come back again." Then the father parted with him to the two men for a handsome bit of money. "Where do you want to sit?" they said to him. "Oh, just set me on the rim of your hat, and then I can walk backwards and forwards and look at the country, and still not fall down." They did as he wished, and when Thumbling had taken leave of his father, they went away with him. They walked until it was dusk, and then the little fellow said, "Do take me down; I want to come down." The man took his hat off, and put the little fellow on the ground by the wayside, and he leapt and crept about a little between the sods, and then he suddenly slipped into a mouse-hole which he had sought out. "Good-evening, gentlemen, just go home without me," he cried to them, and mocked them. They ran thither and stuck their sticks into the mouse-hole, but it was all lost labor. Thumbling crept still farther in, and as it soon became quite dark, they were forced to go home with their vexation and their empty purses.

When Thumbling saw that they were gone, he crept back out of the subterranean passage. "It is so dangerous to walk on the ground in the dark," said he; "how easily a neck or a leg is broken!" Fortunately, he knocked against an empty snail-shell. "Thank God!" said he. "In that I can pass the night in safety," and got into it. Not long afterwards, when he was just going to sleep, he heard two men go by, and one of them was saying, "How shall we contrive to get hold of the rich pastor's silver and gold?" "I could tell you that," cried Thumbling, interrupting them. "What was that?" said one of the thieves in a fright; "I heard some one speaking." They stood still listening, and Thumbling spoke again and said, "Take me with you, and I'll help you."

"But where are you?" "Just look on the ground, and observe from where my voice comes," he replied. There the thieves at length found him, and lifted him up. "You little imp, how will you help us?" they said. "A great deal," said he; "I will creep into the pastor's room through the iron bars, and will reach out to you whatever you want to have." "Come, then," they said, "and we will see what you can do." When they got to the pastor's house, Thumbling crept into the room, but instantly cried out with all his might, "Do you want to have everything that is here?" The thieves were alarmed, and said, "But do speak softly, so as not to waken any one!" Thumbling, however, behaved as if he had not understood this, and cried again, "What do you want? Do you want to have everything that is here?" The cook, who slept in the next room, heard this and sat up in bed, and listened. The thieves, however, had in their fright run some distance away, but at last they took courage, and thought, "The little rascal wants to mock us." They came back and whispered to him, "Come, be serious, and reach something out to us." Then Thumbling again cried as loudly as he could, "I really will give you everything, only put your hands in." The maid who was listening, heard this quite distinctly, and jumped out of bed and rushed to the door. The thieves took flight, and ran as if the Wild Huntsman were behind them, but as the maid could not see anything, she went to strike a light. When she came to the place with it, Thumbling, unperceived, hid himself in the granary, and the maid, after she had examined every corner and found nothing, lay down in her bed again, and believed that, after all, she had only been dreaming with open eyes and ears.

Thumbling had climbed up among the hay and found a beautiful place to sleep in: there he intended to rest until day, and then go home again to his parents. But he had other things to go through. Truly there is much affliction and misery in this world! When day dawned, the maid arose from her bed to feed the cows. Her first walk was into the barn, where she laid hold of an armful of hay, and precisely that very one in which poor Thumbling was lying asleep. He, however, was sleeping so soundly that he was aware of nothing, and did not awake until he was in the mouth of the cow, who had picked him up with the hay. "Ah, heavens!" cried he, "how have I got into the fulling mill?" but he soon discovered where he was. Then it was necessary to be careful not to let himself go between the teeth and be dismembered, but he was nevertheless forced to slip down into the stomach with the hay. "In this little room the windows are forgotten," said he, "and no sun shines in, neither will a candle be brought." His quarters were especially unpleasing to him, and the worst was, more and more hay was always coming in by the door, and the space grew less and less. Then, at length in his anguish, he cried as loud as he could, "Bring me no more fodder, bring me no more fodder." The maid was just milking the cow, and when she heard some one speaking, and saw no one, and perceived that it was the same voice that she had heard in the night, she was so terrified that she slipped off her stool, and spilt the milk. She ran in the greatest haste to her master, and said, "Oh, heavens, pastor, the cow has been speaking!" "You are mad," replied the pastor; but he went himself to the byre to see what was there. Hardly, however, had he set his foot inside than Thumbling again cried, "Bring me no more fodder, bring me no more fodder." Then the pastor himself was alarmed, and thought that an evil spirit had gone into the cow, and ordered her to be killed. She was killed, but the stomach, in which Thumbling was, was thrown on the midden. Thumbling had great difficulty in working his way out; however, he succeeded so far as to get some room, but, just as he was going to thrust his head out, a new misfortune occurred. A hungry wolf ran thither, and swallowed the whole stomach at one gulp. Thumbling did not lose courage.

"Perhaps," thought he, "the wolf will listen to what I have got to say," and he called to him from out of his stomach, "Dear wolf, I know of a magnificent feast for you."

"Where is it to be had?" said the wolf.

"In such and such a house; you must creep into it through the kitchen-sink; you will find cakes, and bacon, and sausages, and as much of them as you can eat," and he described to him exactly his father's house. The wolf did not require to be told this twice, squeezed himself in at night through the sink, and ate to his heart's content in the larder. When he had eaten his fill, he wanted to go out again, but he had become so big that he could not go out by the same way. Thumbling had reckoned on this, and now began to make a violent noise in the wolfs body, and raged and screamed as loudly as he could. "Will you be quiet," said the wolf; "you will waken up the people!" "Eh, what," replied the little fellow, "you have eaten your fill, and I will make merry likewise," and began once more to scream with all his strength. At last his father and mother were aroused by it, and ran to the room and looked in through the opening in the door. When they saw that a wolf was inside, they ran away, and the husband fetched his axe, and the wife the scythe. "Stay behind," said the man, when they entered the room. "When I have given him a blow, if he is not killed by it, you must cut him down and hew his body to pieces." Then Thumbling heard his parents' voices, and cried, "Dear father, I am here; I am in the wolf's body." Said the father, full of joy, "Thank God, our dear child has found us again," and bade the woman take away her scythe, that Thumbling might not be hurt with it. After that he raised his arm, and struck the wolf such a blow on his head that he fell down dead, and then they got knives and scissors and cut his body open, and drew the little fellow forth. "Ah," said the father, "what sorrow we have gone through for your sake." "Yes, father, I have gone about the world a great deal. Thank heaven, I breathe fresh air again!" "Where have you been, then?" "Ah, father, I have been in a mouse's hole, in a cow's stomach, and then in a wolf's; now I will stay with you." "And we will not sell you again; no, not for all the riches in the world," said his parents, and they embraced and kissed their dear Thumbling.

# BRIAR ROSE

Once upon a time there lived a king and queen who had no children; and this they lamented very much. But one day, as the queen was walking by the side of the river, a little fish lifted its head out of the water, and said, "Your wish shall be fulfilled, and you shall soon have a daughter."

What the little fish had foretold soon came to pass; and the queen had a little girl who was so very beautiful that the king could not cease looking on her for joy, and determined to hold a great feast. So he invited not only his relations, friends, and neighbors, but also all the fairies, that they might be kind and good to his little daughter. Now there were thirteen fairies in his kingdom, and he had only twelve golden dishes for them to eat out of, so that he was obliged to leave one of the fairies without an invitation. The rest came, and after the feast was over they gave all their best gifts to the little princess; one gave her virtue, another beauty, another riches, and so on till she had all that was excellent in the world. When eleven had done blessing her, the thirteenth, who had not been invited, and was very angry on that account, came in, and determined to take her revenge. So she cried out, "The king's daughter shall in her fifteenth year be wounded by a spindle, and fall down dead." Then the twelfth, who had not yet given her gift, came forward and said that the bad wish must be fulfilled, but that she could soften it, and that the king's daughter should not die, but fall asleep for a hundred years.

But the king hoped to save his dear child from the threatened evil, and ordered that all the spindles in the kingdom should be bought up and destroyed. All the fairies' gifts were in the meantime fulfilled; for the princess was so beautiful, and well-behaved and amiable, and wise, that every one who knew her loved her.

Now it happened that on the very day she was fifteen years old the king and queen were not at home, and she was left alone in the palace. So she roamed about by herself, and looked at all the rooms and chambers, till at last she came to an old tower, to which there was a narrow staircase ending with a little door. In the door there was a golden key, and when she turned it the door sprang open, and there sat an old lady spinning away very busily.

"Why, how now, good mother," said the princess, "what are you doing there?"

"Spinning," said the old lady, and nodded her head. "How prettily that little thing turns round!" said the princess, and took the spindle and began to spin. But scarcely had she touched it before the prophecy was fulfilled, and she fell down lifeless on the ground.

However, she was not dead, but had only fallen into a deep sleep; and the king and the queen, who just then came home, and all their court, fell asleep too, and the horses slept in the stables, and the dogs in the yard, and the pigeons on the house-top, and the flies on the walls. Even the fire on the I hearth left off blazing, and went to sleep; and the meat that was roasting stood still; and the cook, who was at that moment pulling the kitchen-boy by the hair to give him a box on the ear for something he had done amiss, let him go, and both fell asleep; and so everything stood still, and slept soundly.

A high hedge of thorns soon grew around the palace, and every year it became higher and thicker, till at last the whole palace was surrounded and hidden, so that not even the roof or the chimneys could be seen.

But there went a report through all the land of the beautiful sleeping Briar Rose, for thus was the king's daughter called; so that from time to time several kings' sons came, and tried to break through the thicket into the palace.

This they could never do; for the thorns and bushes laid hold of them as it were with hands, and there they stuck fast and died miserably.

After many, many years there came another king's son into that land, and an old man told him the story of the thicket of thorns, and how a beautiful palace stood behind it, in which was a wondrous princess, called Briar Rose, asleep with all her court. He told, too, how he had heard from his grandfather that many, many princes had come, and had tried to break through the thicket, but had stuck fast and died.

Then the young prince said, "All this shall not frighten me; I will go and see Briar Rose." The old man tried to dissuade him, but he persisted in going.

Now that very day the hundred years were completed; and as the prince came to the thicket he saw nothing but beautiful flowering shrubs, through which he passed with ease, and they closed after him as firm as ever.

Then he came at last to the palace, and there in the yard lay the dogs asleep, and the horses in the stables, and on the roof sat the pigeons fast asleep with their heads under their wings; and when he came into the palace, the flies slept on the walls, and the cook in the kitchen was still holding up her hand as if she would beat the boy, and the maid sat with a black fowl in her hand ready to be plucked.

Then he went on still further, and all was so still that he could hear every breath he drew; till at last he came to the old tower and opened the door of the little room in which Briar Rose was, and there she lay fast asleep, and looked so beautiful that he could not take his eyes off, and he stooped down and gave her a kiss. But the moment he kissed her she opened her eyes and awoke, and smiled upon him.

Then they went out together, and presently the king and queen also awoke, and all the court, and they gazed on each other with great wonder.

And the horses got up and shook themselves, and the dogs jumped about and barked; the pigeons took their heads from under their wings, and looked about and flew into the fields; the flies on the walls buzzed away; the fire in the kitchen blazed up and cooked the dinner, and the roast meat turned round again; the cook gave the boy the box on his ear so that he cried out, and the maid went on plucking the fowl.

And then was the wedding of the prince and Briar Rose celebrated, and they lived happily together all their lives.

# THE SIX SWANS

A King was once hunting in a large wood, and pursued his game so hotly that none of his courtiers could follow him. But when evening approached he stopped, and looking around him perceived that he had lost himself. He sought a path out of the forest but could not find one, and presently he saw an old woman, with a nodding head, who came up to him. "My good woman," said he to her, "can you not show me the way out of the forest?" "Oh, yes, my lord King," she replied; "I can do that very well, but upon one condition, which if you do not fulfil, you will never again get out of the wood, but will die of hunger."

"What, then, is this condition?" asked the King.

"I have a daughter," said the old woman, "who is as beautiful as any one you can find in die whole world, and well deserves to be your bride. Now, if you will make her your Queen, I will show you your way out of the wood." In the anxiety of his heart, the King consented, and the old woman led him to her cottage, where the daughter was sitting by the fire. She received the King as if she had expected him, and he saw at once that she was very beautiful, but yet she did not quite please him, for he could not look at her without a secret shuddering. However, he took the maiden upon his horse, and the old woman showed him the way, and the King arrived safely at his palace, where the wedding was to be celebrated.

The King had been married once before, and had seven children by his first wife, six boys and a girl, whom he loved above everything else in the world. He became afraid, soon, that the step-mother might not treat his children very well, and might even do them some great injury, so he took them away to a lonely castle which stood in the midst of a forest. The castle was so entirely hidden, and the way to it was so difficult to discover, that he himself could not have found it if a wise woman had not given him a ball of cotton which had the wonderful property, when he threw it before him, of unrolling itself and showing him the right path. The King went, however, so often to see his dear children, that the Queen, noticing his absence, became inquisitive, and wished to know what he went to fetch out of the forest. So she gave his servants a great quantity of money, and they disclosed to her the secret, and also told her of the ball of cotton which alone could show her the way. She had now no peace until she discovered where this ball was concealed, and then she made some fine silken shirts, and, as she had learnt of her mother, she sewed within each a charm. One day soon after, when the King was gone out hunting, she took the little shirts and went into the forest, and the cotton showed her the path. The children, seeing some one coming in the distance, thought it was their dear father, and ran out full of joy. Then she threw over each of them a shirt, that, as it touched their bodies, changed them into Swans, which flew away over the forest. The Queen then went home quite contented, and thought she was free of her step-children; but the little girl had not met her with the brothers, and the Queen did not know of her.

The following day the King went to visit his children, but he found only the Maiden. "Where are your brothers?" asked he. "Ah, dear father," she replied, "they are gone away and have left me alone"; and she told him how she had looked out of the window and seen them changed into Swans, which had flown over the forest; and then she showed him the feathers which they had dropped in the courtyard, and which she had collected together. The King was much grieved, but he did not think that his wife could have done this wicked deed, and, as he feared the girl might also be stolen away, he took her with him. She was, however, so much afraid of the step-mother, that she begged him not to stop more than one night in the castle.

The poor Maiden thought to herself, "This is no longer my place; I will go and seek my brothers"; and when night came she escaped and went quite deep into the wood. She walked all night long, and a great part of the next day, until she could go no further from weariness. Just then she saw a rough-looking hut, and going in, she found a room with six little beds, but she dared not get into one, so crept under, and laying herself upon the hard earth, prepared to pass the night there. Just as the sun was setting, she heard a rustling, and saw six white Swans come flying in at the window. They settled on the ground and began blowing one another until they had blown all their feathers off, and their swan's down slipped from them like a shirt. Then the Maiden knew them at once for her brothers, and gladly crept out from under the bed, and the brothers were not less glad to see their sister, but their joy was of short duration. "Here you must not stay," said they to her; "this is a robbers' hiding-place; if they should return and find you here, they would murder you."

"Can you not protect me, then?" inquired the sister.

"No," they replied; "for we can only lay aside our swan's feathers for a quarter of an hour each evening, and for that time we regain our human form, but afterwards we resume our changed appearance."

Their sister then asked them, with tears, "Can you not be restored again?"

"Oh, no," replied they; "the conditions are too difficult. For six long years you must neither speak nor laugh, and during that time you must sew together for us six little shirts of star-flowers, and should there fall a single word from your lips, then all your labor will be in vain." Just as the brothers finished speaking, the quarter of an hour elapsed, and they all flew out of the window again like Swans.

The little sister, however, made a solemn resolution to rescue her brothers, or die in the attempt; and she left the cottage, and, penetrating deep into the forest, passed the night amid the branches of a tree. The next morning she went out and collected the star-flowers to sew together. She had no one to converse with and for laughing she had no spirits, so there up in the tree she sat, intent upon her work.

After she had passed some time there, it happened that the King of that country was hunting in the forest, and his huntsmen came beneath the tree on which the Maiden sat. They called to her and asked, "Who art thou?" But she gave no answer. "Come down to us," continued they; "we will do thee no harm." She simply shook her head, and when they pressed her further with questions, she threw down to them her gold necklace, hoping therewith to satisfy them. They did not, however, leave her, and she threw down her girdle, but in vain! and even her rich dress did not make them desist. At last the huntsman himself climbed the tree and brought down the Maiden, and took her before the King.

The King asked her, "Who art thou? What dost thou upon that tree?" But she did not answer; and then he questioned her in all the languages that he knew, but she remained dumb to all, as a fish. Since, however, she was so beautiful, the King's heart was touched, and he conceived for her a strong affection. Then he put around her his cloak, and, placing her before him on his horse, took her to his castle. There he ordered rich clothing to be made for her, and, although her beauty shone as the sunbeams, not a word escaped her. The King placed her by his side at table, and there her dignified mien and manners so won upon him, that he said, "This Maiden will I marry, and no other in the world;" and after some days he wedded her.

Now, the King had a wicked step-mother, who was discontented with his marriage, and spoke evil of the young Queen. "Who knows whence the wench comes?" said she. "She who cannot speak is not worthy of a King." A year after, when the Queen brought her first-born into the world, the old woman took him away. Then she went to the King and complained that the Queen was a murderess. The King, however, would not believe it, and suffered no one to do any injury to his wife, who sat composedly sewing at her shirts and paying attention to nothing else. When a second child was born, the false stepmother used the same deceit, but the King again would not listen to her words, saying, "She is too pious and good to act so; could she but speak and defend herself, her innocence would come to light." But when again, the old woman stole away the third child, and then accused the Queen, who answered not a word to the accusation, the King was obliged to give her up to be tried, and she was condemned to suffer death by fire.

When the time had elapsed, and the sentence was to be carried out, it happened that the very day had come round when her dear brothers should be set free; the six shirts were also ready, all but the last, which yet wanted the left sleeve. As she was led to the scaffold, she placed the shirts upon her arm, and just as she had mounted it, and the fire was about to be kindled, she looked around, and saw six Swans come flying through the air. Her heart leapt for joy as she perceived her deliverers approaching, and soon the Swans, flying towards her, alighted so near that she was enabled to throw over them the shirts, and as soon as she had done so, their feathers fell off and the brothers stood up alive and well; but the youngest was without his left arm, instead of which he had a swan's wing. They embraced and kissed each other, and the Queen, going to the King, who was thunderstruck, began to say, "Now may I speak, my dear husband, and prove to you that I am innocent and falsely accused;" and then she told him how the wicked woman had stolen away and hidden her three children. When she had concluded, the King was overcome with joy, and the wicked stepmother was led to the scaffold and bound to the stake and burnt to ashes. The King and Queen for ever after lived in peace and prosperity with their six brothers.

## RAPUNZEL

There were once a man and a woman who had long in in vain wished for a child. At length the woman hoped that God was about to grant her desire. These people had a little window at the back of their house from which a splendid garden could be seen, which was full of the most beautiful flowers and herbs. It was, however, surrounded by a high wall, and no one dared to go into it because it belonged to an enchantress, who had great power and was dreaded by all the world. One day the woman was standing by this window and looking down into the garden, when she saw a bed which was planted with the most beautiful rampion (rapunzel), and it looked so fresh and green that she longed for it, and had the greatest desire to eat some. This desire increased every day, and as she knew that she could not get any of it, she quite pined away, and looked pale and miserable. Then her husband was alarmed, and asked, "What ails you, dear wife?" "Ah," she replied, "if I can't get some of the rampion which is in the garden behind our house, to eat, I shall die." The man, who loved her, thought, "Sooner than let your wife die, bring her some of the rampion yourself, let it cost you what it will." In the twilight of evening, he clambered down over the wall into the garden of the enchantress, hastily clutched a handful of rampion, and took it to his wife. She at once made herself a salad of it, and ate it with much relish. She, however, liked it so much, so very much, that the next day she longed for it three times as much as before. If he was to have any rest, her husband must once more descend into the garden. In the gloom of evening, therefore, he let himself down again; but when he had clambered down the wall he was terribly afraid, for he saw the enchantress standing before him. "How can you dare," said she with angry look, "to descend into my garden and steal my rampion like a thief? You shall suffer for it!" "Ah," answered he, "let mercy take the place of justice. I only made up my mind to do it out of necessity. My wife saw your rampion from the window, and felt such a longing for it that she would have died if she had not got some to eat." Then the enchantress allowed her anger to be softened, and said to him, "If the case be as you say, I will allow you to take away with you as much rampion as you will, only I make one condition, you must give me the child which your wife will bring into the world; it shall be well treated, and I will care for it like a mother." The man in his terror consented to everything, and when the little one came to them, the enchantress appeared at once, gave the child the name of Rapunzel, and took it away with her.

Rapunzel grew into the most beautiful child beneath the sun. When she was twelve years old, the enchantress shut her into a tower, which lay in a forest, and had neither stairs nor door, but quite at the top was a little window. When the enchantress wanted to go in, she placed herself beneath this, and cried,

> "Rapunzel, Rapunzel,
> Let down your hair to me."

Rapunzel had magnificent long hair, fine as spun gold, and when she heard the voice of the enchantress she unfastened her braided tresses, wound them round one of the hooks of the window above, and then the hair fell twenty yards down, and the enchantress climbed up by it.

After a year or two, it came to pass that the King's son rode through the forest and went by the tower. Then he heard a song, which was so charming that he stood still and listened. This was Rapunzel, who in her solitude passed her time in letting her sweet voice resound. The King's son wanted to climb up to her, and looked for the door of the tower, but none was to be found. He rode home, but the singing had so deeply touched his heart, that every day he went out into the forest and listened to it. Once when he was thus standing behind a tree, he saw that an enchantress came there, and he heard how she cried,

> "Rapunzel, Rapunzel,
> Let down your hair."

Then Rapunzel let down the braids of her hair, and the enchantress climbed up to her. "If that is the ladder by which one mounts, I will for once try my fortune," said he, and the next day, when it began to grow dark, he went to the tower and cried.

"Rapunzel, Rapunzel,
Let down your hair."

Immediately the hair fell down, and the King's son climbed up.

At first Rapunzel was terribly frightened when a man such as her eyes had never yet beheld came to her; but the King's son began to talk to her quite like a friend, and told her that his heart had been so stirred that it had let him have no rest, and he had been forced to see her. Then Rapunzel lost her fear, and when he asked her if she would take him for a husband, and she saw that he was young and handsome, she thought, "He will love me more than old Dame Gothel does;" and she said yes, and laid her hand in his. She said, "I will willingly go away with you, but I do not know how to get down. Bring with you a skein of silk every time that you come, and I will weave a ladder with it, and when that is ready I will descend, and you will take me on your horse." They agreed that until that time he should come to her every evening, for the old woman came by day. The enchantress remarked nothing of this, until once Rapunzel said to her, "Tell me, Dame Gothel, how it happens that you are so much heavier for me to draw up than the young King's son—he is with me in a moment." "Ah! you wicked child," cried the enchantress, "what do I hear you say! I thought I had separated you from all the world, and yet you have deceived me!" In her anger she clutched Rapunzel's beautiful tresses, wrapped them twice round her left hand, seized a pair of scissors with the right, and snip, snip, they were cut off, and the lovely braids lay on the ground. And she was so pitiless that she took poor Rapunzel into a desert, where she had to live in great grief and misery.

On the same day, however, that she cast out Rapunzel, the enchantress in the evening fastened the braids of hair which she had cut off to the hook of the window, and when the King's son came and cried,

"Rapunzel, Rapunzel,
Let down your hair,"

she let the hair down. The King's son ascended, but he did not find his dearest Rapunzel above, but the enchantress, who gazed at him with wicked and venomous looks. "Aha!" she cried mockingly. "You would fetch your dearest, but the beautiful bird sits no longer singing in the nest; the cat has got it, and will scratch out your eyes as well. Rapunzel is lost to you; you will never see her more." The King's son was beside himself with pain, and in his despair he leapt down from the tower. He escaped with his life, but the thorns into which he fell pierced his eyes. Then he wandered quite blind about the forest, ate nothing but roots and berries, and did nothing but lament and weep over the loss of his dearest wife. Thus he roamed about I in misery for some years, and at length came to the desert where Rapunzel lived in wretchedness. He heard a voice, and it seemed so familiar to him that he went towards it, and when he approached, Rapunzel knew him and fell on his neck and wept. Two of her tears wetted his eyes, and they grew clear again, and he could see with them as before. He led her to his kingdom, where he was joyfully received, and they lived for a long time afterwards, happy and contented.

# MOTHER HOLLE

There was once a widow who had two daughters—one of whom was pretty and industrious, while the other was ugly and idle. But she was much fonder of the ugly and idle one, because she was her own daughter; and the other, who was a step-daughter, was obliged to do all the work, and be the Cinderella of the house. Every day the poor girl had to sit by a well, in the highway, and spin and spin till her fingers bled.

Now it happened that one day the shuttle was marked with her blood, so she dipped it in the well, to wash the mark off; but it dropped out of her hand and fell to the bottom. She began to weep, and ran to her step-mother and told of the mishap. But she scolded her sharply, and was so merciless as to say, "Since you have let the shuttle fall in, you must fetch it out again."

So the girl went back to the well, and did not know what to do; and in the sorrow of her heart she jumped into the well to get the shuttle. She lost her senses; and when she awoke and came to herself again, she was in a lovely meadow where the sun was shining and many thousands of flowers were growing. Along this meadow she went, and at last came to a baker's oven full of bread, and the bread cried out, "Oh, take me out! take me out! or I shall burn; I have been baked a long time!" So she went up to it, and took out all the loaves one after another with the bread-shovel. After that she went on till she came to a tree covered with apples, which called out to her, "Oh, shake me! shake me! we apples are all ripe!" So she shook the tree till the apples fell like rain, and went on shaking till they were all down, and when she had gathered them into a heap, she went on her way.

At last she came to a little house, out of which an old woman peeped; but she had such large teeth that the girl was frightened, and was about to run away.

But the old woman called out to her, "What are you afraid of, dear child? Stay with me; if you will do all the work in the house properly, you shall be the better for it. Only you must take care to make my bed well, and to shake it thoroughly till the feathers fly—for then there is snow on the earth. I am Mother Holle."

As the old woman spoke so kindly to her, the girl took courage and agreed to enter her service. She attended to everything to the satisfaction of her mistress, and always shook her bed so vigorously that the feathers flew about like snow-flakes. So she had a pleasant life with her; never an angry word; and boiled or roast meat every day.

She stayed some time with Mother Holle, and then she became sad. At first she did not know what was the matter with her, but found at length that it was homesickness; although she was many times better off here than at home, still she had a longing to be there. At last she said to the old woman, "I have a longing for home; and however well off I am down here, I cannot stay any longer; I must go up again to my own people." Mother Holle said, "I am pleased that you long for your home again, and as you have served me so truly, I myself will take you up again." Thereupon she took her by the hand, and led her to a large door. The door was opened, and just as the maiden was standing beneath the doorway, a heavy shower of golden rain fell, and all the gold remained sticking to her, so that she was completely covered with it.

"You shall have that because you are so industrious," said Mother Holle; and at the same time she gave her back the shuttle which she had let fall into the well. Thereupon the door closed, and the maiden found herself up above upon the earth, not far from her mother's house.

And as she went into the yard the cock cried: "Cock-a-doodle-doo! Your golden girl's come back to you!"

So she went in to her mother, and as she arrived thus covered with gold, she was well received, both by her and her sister.

The girl told all that had happened to her; and as soon as the mother heard how she had come by so much wealth, she was very anxious to obtain the same good luck for the ugly and lazy daughter. She had to seat herself by the well and spin; and in order that her shuttle might be stained with blood, she stuck her hand into a thorn-bush and pricked her finger. Then she threw her shuttle into the well, and jumped in after it.

She came, like the other, to the beautiful meadow and walked along the very same path. When she got to the oven the bread again cried, "Oh, take me out! take me out! or I shall burn; I have been baked a long time!" But the lazy thing answered, "As if I had any wish to make myself dirty!" and on she went. Soon she came to the apple-tree, which cried, "Oh, shake me! shake me! we apples are all ripe!" But she answered, "I like that! one of you might fall on my head," and so went on.

When she came to Mother Holle's house she was not afraid, for she had already heard of her big teeth, and she hired herself to her immediately.

The first day she forced herself to work diligently, and obeyed Mother Holle when she told her to do anything, for she was thinking of all the gold that she would give her. But on the second day she began to be lazy, and on the third day still more so, and then she would not get up in the morning at all. Neither did she make Mother Holle's bed as she ought, and did not shake it so as to make the feathers fly up. Mother Holle was soon tired of this, and gave her notice to leave. The lazy girl was willing enough to go, and thought that now the golden rain would come. Mother Holle led her, too, to the great door; but while she was standing beneath it, instead of the gold a big kettleful of pitch was emptied over her. "That is the reward of your service," said Mother Holle, and shut the door.

So the lazy girl went home; but she was quite covered with pitch, and the cock by the well-side, as soon as he saw her, cried: "Cock-a-doodle-doo! Your pitchy girl's come back to you." But the pitch stuck fast to her, and could not be got off as long as she lived.

# THE FROG PRINCE

In the olden time, when wishing was having, there lived a King, whose daughters were all beautiful; but the youngest was so exceedingly beautiful that the Sun himself, although he saw her very, very often, was delighted every time she came out into the sunshine.

Near the castle of this King was a large and gloomy forest, where in the midst stood an old lime-tree, beneath whose branches splashed a little fountain; so, whenever it was very hot, the King's youngest daughter ran off into this wood, and sat down by the side of the fountain; and, when she felt dull, would often divert herself by throwing a golden ball up into the air and catching it again. And this was her favorite amusement.

Now, one day it happened that this golden ball, when the King's daughter threw it into the air, did not fall down into her hand, but on to the grass; and then it rolled right into the fountain. The King's daughter followed the ball with her eyes, but it disappeared beneath the water, which was so deep that she could not see to the bottom. Then she began to lament, and to cry more loudly and more loudly; and, as she cried, a voice called out, "Why weepest thou, O King's daughter? thy tears would melt even a stone to pity." She looked around to the spot whence the voice came, and saw a frog stretching his thick, ugly head out of the water. "Ah! you old water-paddler," said she, "was it you that spoke? I am weeping for my golden ball which bounced away from me into the water."

"Be quiet, and do not cry," replied the Frog; "I can give thee good assistance. But what wilt thou give me if I succeed in fetching thy plaything up again?"

"What would you like, dear Frog?" said she. "My dresses, my pearls and jewels, or the golden crown which I wear?"

The Frog replied, "Dresses, or jewels, or golden crowns, are not for me; but if thou wilt love me, and let me be thy companion and playmate, and sit at thy table, and eat from thy little golden plate, and drink out of thy cup, and sleep in thy little bed,—if thou wilt promise me all these things, then I will dive down and fetch up thy golden ball."

"Oh, I will promise you all," said she, "if you will only get me my golden ball." But she thought to herself, "What is the silly Frog chattering about? Let him stay in the water with his equals; he cannot enter into society." Then the Frog, as soon as he had received her promise, drew his head under the water and dived down. Presently he swam up again with the golden ball in his mouth, and threw it on to the grass. The King's daughter was full of joy when she again saw her beautiful plaything; and, taking it up, she ran off immediately. "Stop! stop!" cried the Frog; "take me with thee. I cannot run as thou canst."

But this croaking was of no avail; although it was loud enough, the King's daughter did not hear it, but, hastening home, soon forgot the poor Frog, who was obliged to leap back into the fountain.

The next day, when the King's daughter was sitting at table with her father and all his courtiers, and was eating from her own little golden plate, something was heard coming up the marble stairs, splish-splash, splish-splash; and when it arrived at the top, it knocked at the door, and a voice said—

"Open the door, thou youngest daughter of the King!"

So she arose and went to see who it was that called to her; but when she opened the door and caught sight of the Frog, she shut it again very quickly and with great passion, and sat down at the table, looking exceedingly pale.

But the King perceived that her heart was beating violently, and asked her whether it were a giant who had come to fetch her away who stood at the door. "Oh, no!" answered she; "it is no giant, but an ugly Frog."

"What does the Frog want with you?" said the King.

"Oh, dear father, yesterday when I was playing by the fountain, my golden ball fell into the water, and this Frog fetched it up again because I cried so much: but first, I must tell you, he pressed me so much, that I promised him he should be my companion. I never thought that he could come out of the water, but somehow he has managed to jump out, and now he wants to come in here."

At that moment there was another knock, and a voice said—

"King's daughter, youngest,
Open the door.
Hast thou forgotten
Thy promises made
At the fountain so clear
'Neath the lime-tree's shade?
King's daughter, youngest.
Open the door."

Then the King said, "What you have promised, that you must perform; go and let him in." So the King's daughter went and opened the door, and the Frog hopped in after her right up to her chair: and as soon as she was seated, he said, "Lift me up;" but she hesitated so long that the King had to order her to obey. And as soon as the Frog sat on the chair he jumped on to the table and said, "Now push thy plate near me, that we may eat together." And she did so, but as every one noticed, very unwillingly. The Frog seemed to relish his dinner very much, but every bit that the King's daughter ate nearly choked her, till at last the Frog said, "I have satisfied my hunger, and feel very tired; wilt thou carry me upstairs now into thy chamber, and make thy bed ready that we may sleep together?" At this speech the King's daughter began to cry, for she was afraid of the cold Frog, and dared not touch him; and besides, he actually wanted to sleep in her own beautiful, clean bed!

But her tears only made the King very angry, and he said, "He who helped you in the time of your trouble must not now be despised!" So she took the Frog up with two fingers, and put him into a corner of her chamber. But as she lay in her bed, he crept up to it, and said, "I am so very tired that I shall sleep well; do take me up, or I will tell thy father." This speech put the King's daughter into a terrible passion, and catching the Frog up, she threw him with all her strength against the wall, saying "Now will you be quiet, you ugly Frog!"

But as he fell he was changed from a Frog into a handsome Prince with beautiful eyes, who after a little while became her dear companion and betrothed. One morning, Henry, trusted servant of the Prince, came for them with a carriage. When his master was changed into a frog, trusty Henry had grieved so much that he had bound three iron bands around his heart, for fear it should break with grief and sorrow. The faithful Henry (who was also the trusty Henry) helped in the bride and bridegroom, and placed himself in the seat behind, full of joy at his master's release. They had not proceeded far when the Prince heard a crack as if something had broken behind the carriage; so he put his head out of the window and asked trusty Henry what was broken, and faithful Henry answered, "It was not the carriage, my master, but an iron band which I bound around my heart when it was in such grief because you were changed into a frog."

Twice afterwards on the journey there was the same noise, and each time the Prince thought that it was some part of the carriage that had given way; but it was only the breaking of the bands which bound the heart of the trusty Henry (who was also the faithful Henry), and who was thenceforward free and happy.

# THE TRAVELS OF TOM THUMB

There lived a tailor who had only one son, and he was extremely small, not any larger than your thumb, and so was called Tom Thumb.

However, he was a courageous little fellow, and he told his father, "Father, I am determined to go into the world to seek my fortune."

"Very well, my son," answered the old man, and taking a big darning needle, he made a top to it of sealing wax, and gave it to Tom Thumb, saying:

"There is a sword for you to use to defend yourself on your journeyings."

Then the little fellow, desiring to dine once more with his parents, popped into the kitchen to find out what his mother was preparing for his last dinner at home. All the dishes were ready to be taken in, and they were standing upon the hearth.

"What is it you have for dinner, dear mother?" he inquired.

"You can look for yourself," she replied.

Then Tom sprang up on to the hob, and peeped into all the dishes, but over one he leant so far, that he was carried up by the steam through the chimney, and then for some distance he floated on the smoke, but after a while he fell upon the ground once more.

Now, at last, Tom Thumb was really out in the wide world, and he went on cheerily, and after a time was engaged by a master tailor; but here the food was not so good as his mother's, and it was not to his taste.

So he said, "Mistress, if you will not give me better things to eat, I shall chalk upon your door, 'Too many potatoes, and not enough meat. Good-bye, potato-mill.'"

"I should like to know what you want, you little grasshopper!" cried the woman very angrily, and she seized a shred of cloth to strike him; however, the tiny tailor popped under a thimble, and from it he peeped, putting out his tongue at the mistress.

So she took up the thimble, meaning to catch him, but Tom Thumb hid himself amongst the shreds of cloth, and when she began to search through those, he slipped into a crack in the table, but put out his head to laugh at her; so she tried again to hit him with the shred, but did not succeed in doing so, for he slipped through the crack into the table drawer.

At last, though, he was caught, and driven out of the house.

So the little fellow continued his travels, and presently entering a thick forest, he encountered a company of robbers who were plotting to steal the king's treasure.

As soon as they saw the little tailor, they said to themselves, "A little fellow like this could creep through a keyhole, and aid us greatly." So one called out—

"Hullo, little man, will you come with us to the king's treasury? Certainly a Goliath like you could creep in with ease, and throw out the coins to us."

After considering awhile, Tom Thumb consented, and accompanied them to the king's treasury.

From top to bottom they inspected the door to discover a crack large enough for him to get through, and soon found one. He was for going in directly, but one of the sentinels happening to catch sight of him, exclaimed: "Here is indeed an ugly spider; I will crush it with my foot."

"Leave the poor creature alone," the other said; "it has not done you any harm."

So Tom Thumb slipped through the crack, and made his way to the treasury. Then he opened the window, and cast out the coins to the robbers who were waiting below. While the little tailor was engaged in this exciting employment, he heard the king coming to inspect his treasure, so as quickly as possible he crept out of sight. The king noticed that his treasure had been disarranged, and soon observed that coins were missing: but he was utterly unable to think how they could have been stolen, for the locks and bolts had not been tampered with, and everything was well fastened.

On going from the treasury, he warned the two sentinels, saying—

"Be on the watch, some one is after the money," and quite soon, on Tom Thumb setting to work again, they heard very clearly the coins ringing, chink, chank, as they struck one against the other.

As quickly as possible they unfastened the building and went in, hoping to take the thief.

But Tom Thumb was too quick for them, he sprang into a corner, and hiding himself behind a coin, so that nothing of him was visible, he made fun of the sentinels; crying "I am here!" Then when the men hurried to the spot where the voice came from, he was no longer there, but from a different place cried out: "Ha, Ha! here I am!"

So the sentinels kept jumping about, but so cleverly did Tom move from one spot to another, that they were obliged to run around the whole time, hoping to find somebody, until at length, quite tired out, they went off.

Then Tomb Thumb went on with his work, and one after another he threw all the coins out of the window, but the very last he sounded and rang with all his might and springing nimbly upon it, so flew through the window.

The robbers were loud in their praises.

"Indeed you are a brave fellow," they said, "will you be our captain?"

Tom Thumb, thanking them, declined this honor, for he was anxious to see more of the world. Then the booty was apportioned out, but only a ducat was given to the little tailor, for that was as much as he could carry.

So Tom girded on his sword again, and bidding farewell to the robbers, continued his travels.

He tried to get work under various masters, but they would have nothing to do with him, so after a while he took service at an inn. But the maids there disliked him, for he was about everywhere, and saw all that went on, without being seen himself; and he told their mistress of their dishonest ways, of what was taken off the plates, and from out the cellars.

So they threatened they would drown him, if they caught him, and determined to do him some harm. Then, one day, a maid mowing in the garden saw Tom Thumb running in and out between the blades of grass, so she cut the grass, in great haste, just where he chanced to be, tied it all in a bundle, and, without anyone knowing, threw it to the cows.

Then one big black cow took up a mouthful of grass directly, with Tom in it, and swallowed it down; without doing him any damage, however.

But Tom did not approve of his position, for it was pitch dark down there, with no light burning.

When milking time came, he shouted—

> "Drip, drap, drop,
> Will the milking soon stop?"

but the sound of the milk trickling into the pail prevented his voice being heard.

Not long afterwards the master came into the shed, and said:

"I will have that cow killed to-morrow."

This put Tom Thumb into a great fright, and he called out loudly:

"Please let me out, here I am inside."

This the master heard plainly enough, but could not make out where the voice came from.

"Where are you?" he inquired.

"In the black cow," was the reply.

However, the master could not understand what was meant, and so went away.

The following morning the cow was killed, but fortunately in the cutting up the knife did not touch Tom Thumb, who was put aside with the meat that was to be made into sausages.

When the butcher began chopping, he cried as loudly as he could—

"Don't chop far, I am down beneath," but the chopper made so much noise, that he attracted no attention.

It was indeed a terrible situation for poor Tom. But being in danger brightens one's wits, and he sprang so nimbly, this way and that, keeping clear of the chopper, that not a blow struck him, and he did not get even a scratch.

However, he could not escape, there was no help for it, he was forced into a skin with the sausage meat, so was compelled to make himself as comfortable as might be. It was very close quarters, and besides that, the sausages were suspended to smoke in the chimney, which was by no means entertaining, and the time passed slowly.

When winter came, he was taken down for a guest's meal, and while the hostess was slicing the sausage he had to be on his guard, lest if he stretched out his head it might be cut off.

Watching his opportunity, at last he was able to jump out of the sausage, and right glad was he to be once again in the company of his fellow-men.

It was not very long, however, that he stayed in this house, where he had been met by so many misfortunes, and again he set forth on his travels, rejoicing in his freedom, but this did not long continue.

Swiftly running across the field came a fox, who, in an instant, had snapped up poor little Tom.

"Oh, Mr. Fox," called out the little tailor, "it is I who am in your throat; please let me out."

"Certainly," answered Reynard, "you are not a bit better than nothing at all, you don't in the least satisfy me; make me a promise, that I shall have the hens in your father's yard, and you shall regain your liberty."

"Willingly, you shall have all the hens; I make you a faithful promise," responded Tom Thumb.

So the fox coughed and set him free, and himself carried Tom home.

Then when the father had his dear little son once more he gave the fox all his hens, with the greatest of pleasure.

"Here, father, I am bringing you a golden coin from my travels," said the little fellow, and he brought out the ducat the thieves had apportioned to him.

"But how was it that the fox was given all the poor little hens?"

"Foolish little one, don't you think your father would rather have you, than all the hens he ever had in his yard?"

# SNOW-WHITE AND ROSE-RED

A poor widow once lived in a little cottage. In front of the cottage was a garden, in which were growing two rose trees; one of these bore white roses, and the other red.

She had two children, who resembled the rose trees. One was called Snow-White, and the other Rose-Red; and they were as religious and loving, busy and untiring, as any two children ever were.

Snow-White was more gentle, and quieter than her sister, who liked better skipping about the fields, seeking flowers, and catching summer birds; while Snow-White stayed at home with her mother, either helping her in her work, or, when that was done, reading aloud.

The two children had the greatest affection the one for the other. They were always seen hand in hand; and should Snow-White say to her sister, "We will never separate," the other would reply, "Not while we live," the mother adding, "That which one has, let her always share with the other."

They constantly ran together in the woods, collecting ripe berries; but not a single animal would have injured them; quite the reverse, they all felt the greatest esteem for the young creatures. The hare came to eat parsley from their hands, the deer grazed by their side, the stag bounded past them unheeding; the birds, likewise, did not stir from the bough, but sang in entire security. No mischance befell them; if benighted in the wood, they lay down on the moss to repose and sleep till the morning; and their mother was satisfied as to their safety, and felt no fear about them.

Once, when they had spent the night in the wood, and the bright sunrise awoke them, they saw a beautiful child, in a snow-white robe, shining like diamonds, sitting close to the spot where they had reposed. She arose when they opened their eyes, and looked kindly at them; but said no word, and passed from their sight into the wood. When the children looked around they saw they had been sleeping on the edge of a precipice, and would surely have fallen over if they had gone forward two steps further in the darkness. Their mother said the beautiful child must have been the angel who keeps watch over good children.

Snow-White and Rose-Red kept their mother's cottage so clean that it gave pleasure only to look in. In summer-time Rose-Red attended to the house, and every morning, before her mother awoke, placed by her bed a bouquet which had in it a rose from each of the rose-trees. In winter-time Snow-White set light to the fire, and put on the kettle, after polishing it until it was like gold for brightness. In the evening, when snow was falling, her mother would bid her bolt the door, and then, sitting by the hearth, the good widow would read aloud to them from a big book while the little girls were spinning. Close by them lay a lamb, and a white pigeon, with its head tucked under its wing, was on a perch behind.

One evening, as they were all sitting cosily together like this, there was a knock at the door, as if someone wished to come in.

"Make haste, Rose-Red!" said her mother; "open the door; it is surely some traveller seeking shelter." Rose-Red accordingly pulled back the bolt, expecting to see some poor man. But it was nothing of the kind; it was a bear, that thrust his big, black head in at the open door. Rose-Red cried out and sprang back, the lamb bleated, the dove fluttered her wings, and Snow-White hid herself behind her mother's bed. The bear began speaking, and said, "Do not be afraid; I will not do you any harm; I am half-frozen and would like to warm myself a little at your fire."

"Poor bear!" the mother replied; "come in and lie by the fire; only be careful that your hair is not burnt." Then she called Snow-White and Rose-Red, telling them that the bear was kind, and would not harm them. They came, as she bade them, and presently the lamb and the dove drew near also without fear.

"Children," begged the bear; "knock some of the snow off my coat." So they brought the broom and brushed the bear's coat quite clean.

After that he stretched himself out in front of the fire, and pleased himself by growling a little, only to show that he was happy and comfortable. Before long they were all quite good friends, and the children began to play with their unlooked-for visitor, pulling his thick fur, or placing their feet on his back, or rolling him over and over. Then they took a slender hazel-twig, using it upon his thick coat, and they laughed when he growled. The bear permitted them to amuse themselves in this way, only occasionally calling out, when it went a little too far, "Children, spare me an inch of life."

When it was night, and all were making ready to go to bed, the widow told the bear, "You may stay here and lie by the hearth, if you like, so that you will be sheltered from the cold and from the bad weather."

The offer was accepted, but when morning came, as the day broke in the east, the two children let him out, and over the snow he went back into the wood.

After this, every evening at the same time the bear came, lay by the fire, and allowed the children to play with him; so they became quite fond of their curious playmate, and the door was not ever bolted in the evening until he had appeared.

When spring-time came, and all around began to look green and bright, one morning the bear said to Snow-White, "Now I must leave you, and all the summer long I shall not be able to come back."

"Where, then, are you going, dear Bear?" asked Snow-White.

"I have to go to the woods to protect my treasure from the bad dwarfs. In winter-time, when the earth is frozen hard, they must remain underground, and cannot make their way through: but now that the sunshine has thawed the earth they can come to the surface, and whatever gets into their hands, or is brought to their caves, seldom, if ever, again sees daylight."

Snow-White was very sad when she said good-bye to the good-natured beast, and unfastened the door, that he might go; but in going out he was caught by a hook in the lintel, and a scrap of his fur being torn, Snow-White thought there was something shining like gold through the rent: but he went out so quickly that she could not feel certain what it was, and soon he was hidden among the trees.

One day the mother sent her children into the wood to pick up sticks. They found a big tree lying on the ground. It had been felled, and towards the roots they noticed something skipping and springing, which they could not make out, as it was sometimes hidden in the grasses. As they came nearer they could see it was a dwarf, with a shrivelled-up face and a snow-white beard an ell long. The beard was fixed in a gash in the tree trunk, and the tiny fellow was hopping to and fro, like a dog at the end of a string, but he could not manage to free himself. He stared at the children with his red, fiery eyes, and called out, "Why are you standing there? Can't you come and try to help me?"

"What were you doing, little fellow?" inquired Rose-Red.

"Stupid, inquisitive goose!" replied the dwarf; "I meant to split the trunk, so that I could chop it up for kitchen sticks; big logs would burn up the small quantity of food we cook, for people like us do not consume great heaps of food, as you heavy, greedy folk do. The bill-hook I had driven in, and soon I should have done what I required; but the tool suddenly sprang from the cleft, which so quickly shut up again that it caught my handsome white beard; and here I must stop, for I cannot set myself free. You stupid pale-faced creatures! You laugh, do you?"

In spite of the dwarf's bad temper, the girls took all possible pains to release the little man, but without avail, the beard could not be moved, it was wedged too tightly.

"I will run and get someone else," said Rose-Red.

"Idiot!" cried the dwarf. "Who would go and get more people? Already there are two too many. Can't you think of something better?"

"Don't be so impatient," said Snow-White. "I will try to think." She clapped her hands as if she had discovered a remedy, took out her scissors, and in a moment set the dwarf free by cutting off the end of his beard.

Immediately the dwarf felt that he was free he seized a sack full of gold that was hidden amongst the tree's roots, and, lifting it up, grumbled out, "Clumsy creatures, to cut off a bit of my beautiful beard, of which I am so proud! I leave the cuckoos to pay you for what you did." Saying this, he swung the sack across his shoulder, and went off, without even casting a glance at the children.

Not long afterwards the two sisters went to angle in the brook, meaning to catch fish for dinner. As they were drawing near the water they perceived something, looking like a large grasshopper, springing towards the stream, as if it were going in. They hurried up to see what it might be, and found that it was the dwarf. "Where are you going?" said Rose-Red. "Surely you will not jump into the water?"

"I'm not such a simpleton as that!" yelled the little man. "Don't you see that a wretch of a fish is pulling me in?"

The dwarf had been sitting angling from the side of the stream when, by ill-luck, the wind had entangled his beard in his line, and just afterwards a big fish taking the bait, the unamiable little fellow had not sufficient strength to pull it out; so the fish had the advantage, and was dragging the dwarf after it. Certainly, he caught at every stalk and spray near him, but that did not assist him greatly; he was forced to follow all the twistings of the fish, and was perpetually in danger of being drawn into the brook.

The girls arrived just in time. They caught hold of him firmly and endeavored to untwist his beard from the line, but in vain; they were too tightly entangled. There was nothing left but again to make use of the scissors; so they were taken out, and the tangled portion was cut off.

When the dwarf noticed what they were about, he exclaimed in a great rage, "Is this how you damage my beard? Not content with making it shorter before, you are now making it still smaller, and completely spoiling it. I shall not ever dare show my face to my friends. I wish you had missed your way before you took this road." Then he fetched a sack of pearls that lay among the rushes, and, not saying another word, hobbled off and disappeared behind a large stone.

Soon after this it chanced that the poor widow sent her children to the town to purchase cotton, needles, ribbon, and tape. The way to the town ran over a common, on which in every direction large masses of rocks were scattered about. The children's attention was soon attracted to a big bird that hovered in the air. They remarked that, after circling slowly for a time, and gradually getting nearer to the ground, it all of a sudden pounced down amongst a mass of rock. Instantly a heartrending cry reached their ears, and, running quickly to the place, they saw, with horror, that the eagle had seized their former acquaintance, the dwarf, and was just about to carry him off. The kind children did not hesitate for an instant. They took a firm hold of the little man, and strove so stoutly with the eagle for possession of his contemplated prey, that, after much rough treatment on both sides, the dwarf was left in the hands of his brave little friends, and the eagle took to flight.

As soon as the little man had in some measure recovered from his alarm, his small squeaky, cracked voice was heard saying, "Couldn't you have held me more gently? See my little coat; you have rent and damaged it in a fine manner, you clumsy, officious things!" Then he picked up a sack of jewels, and slipped out of sight behind a piece of rock.

The maidens by this time were quite used to his ungrateful, ungracious ways; so they took no notice of it, but went on their way, made their purchases, and then were ready to return to their happy home.

On their way back, suddenly, once more they ran across their dwarf friend. Upon a clear space he had turned out his sack of jewels, so that he could count and admire them, for he had not imagined that anybody would at so late an hour be coming across the common.

The setting sun was shining upon the brilliant stones, and their changing hues and sparkling rays caused the children to pause to admire them also.

"What are you gazing at?" cried the dwarf, at the same time becoming red with rage; "and what are you standing there for, making ugly faces?" It is probable that he might have proceeded in the same complimentary manner, but suddenly a great growl was heard near by them, and a big black bear joined the party. Up jumped the dwarf in extremest terror, but could not get to his hiding-place, the bear was too close to him; so he cried out in very evident anguish—

"Dear Mr. Bear, forgive me, I pray! I will render to you all my treasure. Just see those precious stones lying there! Grant me my life! What would you do with such an insignificant little fellow? You would not notice me between your teeth. See, though, those two children, they would be delicate morsels, and are as plump as partridges; I beg of you to take them, good Mr. Bear, and let me go!"

But the bear would not be moved by his speeches. He gave the ill-disposed creature a blow with his paw, and he lay lifeless on the ground.

Meanwhile the maidens were running away, making off for home as well as they could; but all of a sudden they were stopped by a well-known voice that called out, "Snow-White, Rose-Red, stay! Do not fear. I will accompany you."

The bear quickly came towards them, but, as he reached their side, suddenly the bear-skin slipped to the ground, and there before them was standing a handsome man, completely garmented in gold, who said—

"I am a king's son, who was enchanted by the wicked dwarf lying over there. He stole my treasure, and compelled me to roam the woods transformed into a big bear until his death should set me free. Therefore he has only received a well-deserved punishment."

Some time afterwards Snow-White married the Prince, and Rose-Red his brother.

They shared between them the enormous treasure which the dwarf had collected in his cave.

The old mother spent many happy years with her children.

# THE THREE LITTLE MEN IN THE WOOD

Once upon a time there lived a man, whose wife had died; and a woman, also, who had lost her husband: and this man and this woman had each a daughter. These two maidens were friendly with each other, and used to walk together, and one day they came by the widow's house. Then the widow said to the man's daughter, "Do you hear, tell your father I wish to marry him, and you shall every morning wash in milk and drink wine, but my daughter shall wash in water and drink water." So the girl went home and told her father what the woman had said, and he replied, "What shall I do? Marriage is a comfort, but it is also a torment." At last, as he could come to no conclusion, he drew off his boot and said: "Take this boot, which has a hole in the sole, and go with it out of doors and hang it on the great nail and then pour water into it. If it holds the water, I will again take a wife; but if it runs through, I will not have her." The girl did as he bid her, but the water drew the hole together and the boot became full to overflowing. So she told her father how it had happened, and he, getting up, saw it was quite true; and going to the widow he settled the matter, and the wedding was celebrated.

The next morning, when the two girls arose, milk to wash in and wine to drink were set for the man's daughter, but only water, both for washing and drinking, for the woman's daughter. The second morning, water for washing and drinking stood before both the man's daughter and the woman's; and on the third morning, water to wash in and water to drink were set before the man's daughter, and milk to wash in and wine to drink before the woman's daughter, and so it continued.

Soon the woman conceived a deadly hatred for her step-daughter, and knew not how to behave badly enough to her from day to day. She was envious, too, because her step-daughter was beautiful and lovely, and her own daughter was ugly and hateful.

Once, in the winter-time, when the river was frozen as hard as a stone, and hill and valley were covered with snow, the woman made a cloak of paper, and called the maiden to her and said, "Put on this cloak, and go away into the wood to fetch me a little basketful of strawberries, for I have a wish for some."

"Mercy on us!" said the maiden, "in winter there are no strawberries growing; the ground is frozen, and the snow, too, has covered everything. And why must I go in that paper cloak? It is so cold out of doors that it freezes one's breath even, and if the wind does not blow off this cloak, the thorns will tear it from my body."

"Will you dare to contradict me?" said the step-mother. "Make haste off, and let me not see you again until you have found me a basket of strawberries." Then she gave her a small piece of dry bread, saying, "On that you must subsist the whole day." But she thought—out of doors she will be frozen and starved, so that my eyes will never see her again!

So the girl did as she was told, and put on the paper cloak, and went away with the basket. Far and near there was nothing but snow, and not a green blade was to be seen. When she came to the forest she discovered a little cottage, out of which three little Dwarfs were peeping. The girl wished them good morning, and knocked gently at the door. They called her in, and entering the room, she sat down on a bench by the fire to warm herself, and eat her breakfast. The Dwarfs called out, "Give us some of it!" "Willingly," she replied, and, dividing her bread in two, she gave them half. They asked, "What do you here in the forest, in the winter-time, in this thin cloak?"

"Ah!" she answered, "I must, seek a basketful of strawberries, and I dare not return home until I can take them with me." When she had eaten her bread, they gave her a broom, saying, "Sweep away the snow with this from the back door." But when she was gone out of doors the three Dwarfs said one to another, "What shall we give her, because she is so gentle and good, and has shared her bread with us?" Then said the first, "I grant to her that she shall become more beautiful every day." The second said, "I grant that a piece of gold shall fall out of her mouth for every word she speaks." The third said, "I grant that a King shall come and make her his bride."

Meanwhile, the girl had done as the Dwarf had bidden her, and had swept away the snow from behind the house. And what do you think she found there? Actually, ripe strawberries!

117

which came quite red and sweet up under the snow. So filling her basket in great glee, she thanked the little men and gave them each her hand, and then ran home to take her step-mother what she wished for. As she went in and said "Good evening," a piece of gold fell from her mouth. Thereupon she related what had happened to her in the forest; but at every word she spoke a piece of gold fell, so that the whole floor was covered.

"Just see her arrogance," said the step-sister, "to throw away money in that way!" but in her heart she was jealous, and wished to go into the forest, too, to seek strawberries. Her mother said, "No, my dear daughter; it is too cold, you will be frozen!" but as her girl let her have no peace, she at last consented, and made her a beautiful fur cloak to put on; she also gave her buttered bread and cooked meat to eat on her way.

The girl went into the forest and came straight to the little cottage. The three Dwarfs were peeping out again, but she did not greet them; and, stumbling on without looking at them, or speaking, she entered the room, and, seating herself by the fire, began to eat the bread and butter and meat. "Give us some of that," exclaimed the Dwarfs; but she answered, "I have not got enough for myself, so how can I give any away?" When she had finished they said, "You have a broom there, go and sweep the back door clean." "Oh, sweep it yourself," she replied; "I am not your servant." When she saw that they would not give her anything she went out at the door, and the three Dwarfs said to each other, "What shall we give her? She is so ill-behaved, and has such a bad and envious disposition, that nobody can wish well to her." The first said, "I grant that she becomes more ugly every day." The second said, "I grant that at every word she speaks a toad shall spring out of her mouth." The third said, "I grant that she shall die a miserable death." Meanwhile the girl had been looking for strawberries out of doors, but as she could find none she went home very peevish. When she opened her mouth to tell her mother what had happened to her in the forest, a toad jumped out of her mouth at each word, so that every one fled away from her in horror.

The step-mother was now still more vexed, and was always thinking how she could do the most harm to her husband's daughter, who every day became more beautiful. At last she took a kettle, set it on the fire, and boiled a net therein. When it was sodden she hung it on the shoulder of the poor girl, and gave her an axe, that she might go upon the frozen pond and cut a hole in the ice to drag the net. She obeyed, and went away and cut an ice-hole; and while she was cutting, an elegant carriage came by, in which the King sat. The carriage stopped, and the King asked, "My child, who are you? and what do you here?" "I am a poor girl, and am dragging a net," said she. Then the King pitied her, and saw how beautiful she was, and said, "Will you go with me?" "Yes, indeed, with all my heart," she replied, for she was glad to get out of the sight of her mother and sister.

So she was handed into the carriage, and driven away with the King; and as soon as they arrived at his castle the wedding was celebrated with great splendor, as the Dwarfs had granted to the maiden. After a year the young Queen bore a son; and when the step-mother heard of her great good fortune, she came to the castle with her daughter, and behaved as if she had come on a visit. But one day when the King had gone out, and no one was present, this bad woman seized the Queen by the head, and her daughter caught hold of her feet, and raising her out of bed, they threw her out of the window into the river which ran past. Then, laying her ugly daughter in the bed, the old woman covered her up, even over her head; and when the King came back he wished to speak to his wife, but the old woman exclaimed, "Softly! softly! do not go near her; she is lying in a beautiful sleep, and must be kept quiet to-day." The King, not thinking of an evil design, came again the next morning the first thing; and when he spoke to his wife, and she answered, a toad sprang out of her mouth at every word, as a piece of gold had done before. So he asked what had happened, and the old woman said, "That is produced by her weakness, she will soon lose it again."

But in the night the kitchen-boy saw a Duck swimming through the brook, and the Duck asked:

> *"King, King, what are you doing?*
> Are you sleeping, or are you waking?"

And as he gave no answer, the Duck said:

> *"What are my guests a-doing?"*

Then the boy answered:

> *"They all sleep sound."*

And she asked him:

> *"How fares my child?"*

And he replied:

> *"In his cradle he sleeps."*

Then she came up in the form of the Queen to the cradle, and gave the child drink, shook up his bed, and covered him up, and then swam away again as a duck through the brook. The second night she came again; and on the third she said to the kitchen-boy, "Go and tell the King to take his sword, and swing it thrice over me, on the threshold." Then the boy ran and told the King, who came with his sword, and swung it thrice over the Duck; and at the third time his bride stood before him, bright, living, and healthful, as she had been before.

Now the King was in great happiness, but he hid the Queen in a chamber until the Sunday when the child was to be christened; and when all was finished he asked, "What ought to be done to one who takes another out of a bed and throws her into the river?" "Nothing could be more proper," said the old woman, "than to put such a one into a cask, stuck round with nails, and to roll it down the hill into the water." Then the King said, "You have spoken your own sentence"; and ordering a cask to be fetched, he caused the old woman and her daughter to be put into it, and the bottom nailed up. Then the cask was rolled down the hill until it fell into the water.

# RUMPELSTILTSKIN

There was once a poor Miller who had a beautiful daughter, and one day, having to go to speak with the King, he said, in order to make himself appear of consequence, that he had a daughter who could spin straw into gold. The King was very fond of gold, and thought to himself, "That is an art which would please me very well"; and so he said to the Miller, "If your daughter is so very clever, bring her to the castle in the morning, and I will put her to the proof."

As soon as she arrived the King led her into a chamber which was full of straw; and, giving her a wheel and a reel, he said, "Now set yourself to work, and if you have not spun this straw into gold by an early hour to-morrow, you must die." With these words he shut the room door, and left the maiden alone.

There she sat for a long time, thinking how to save her life; for she understood nothing of the art whereby straw might be spun into gold; and her perplexity increased more and more, till at last she began to weep. All at once the door opened, and in stepped a little Man, who said, "Good evening, fair maiden; why do you weep so sore?" "Ah," she replied, "I must spin this straw into gold, and I am sure I do not know how."

The little Man asked, "What will you give me if I spin it for you?"

"My necklace," said the maiden.

The Dwarf took it, placed himself in front of the wheel, and whirr, whirr, whirr, three times round, and the bobbin was full. Then he set up another, and whir, whir, whir, thrice round again, and a second bobbin was full; and so he went all night long, until all the straw was spun, and the bobbins were full of gold. At sunrise the King came, very much astonished to see the gold; the sight of which gladdened him, but did not make his heart less covetous. He caused the maiden to be led into another room, still larger, full of straw; and then he bade her spin it into gold during the night if she valued her life. The maiden was again quite at a loss what to do; but while she cried the door opened suddenly, as before, and the Dwarf appeared and asked her what she would give him in return for his assistance. "The ring off my finger," she replied. The little Man took the ring and began to spin at once, and by morning all the straw was changed to glistening gold. The King was rejoiced above measure at the sight of this, but still he was not satisfied, but, leading the maiden into another still larger room, full of straw as the others, he said, "This you must spin during the night; but if you accomplish it you shall be my bride." "For," thought he to himself, "a richer wife thou canst not have in all the world."

When the maiden was left alone, the Dwarf again appeared and asked, for the third time, "What will you give me to do this for you?"

"I have nothing left that I can give you," replied the maiden.

"Then promise me your first-born child if you become Queen," said he.

The Miller's daughter thought, "Who can tell if that will ever happen?" and, ignorant how else to help herself out of her trouble, she promised the Dwarf what he desired; and he immediately set about and finished the spinning. When morning came, and the King found all he had wished for done, he celebrated his wedding, and the Miller's fair daughter became Queen.

The gay times she had at the King's Court caused her to forget that she had made a very foolish promise.

About a year after the marriage, when she had ceased to think about the little Dwarf, she brought a fine child into the world; and, suddenly, soon after its birth, the very man appeared and demanded what she had promised. The frightened Queen offered him all the riches of the kingdom if he would leave her her child; but the Dwarf answered, "No; something human is dearer to me than all the wealth of the world."

The Queen began to weep and groan so much that the Dwarf pitied her, and said, "I will leave you three days to consider; if you in that time discover my name you shall keep your child."

All night long the Queen racked her brains for all the names she could think of, and sent a messenger through the country to collect far and wide any new names. The following morning came the Dwarf, and she began with "Caspar," "Melchior," "Balthassar," and all the odd names she knew; but at each the little Man exclaimed, "That is not my name." The second day the Queen inquired of all her people for uncommon and curious names, and called the Dwarf "Ribs-of-Beef," "Sheep-shank," "Whalebone," but at each he said, "This is not my name." The third day the messenger came back and said, "I have not found a single name; but as I came to a high mountain near the edge of a forest, where foxes and hares say good night to each other, I saw there a little house, and before the door a fire was burning, and round this fire a very curious little Man was dancing on one leg, and shouting:

> "'To-day I stew, and then I'll bake,
> To-morrow I shall the Queen's child take;
> Ah! how famous it is that nobody knows
> That my name is Rumpelstiltskin.'"

When the Queen heard this she was very glad, for now she knew the name; and soon after came the Dwarf, and asked, "Now, my lady Queen, what is my name?"

First she said, "Are you called Conrade?" "No."

"Are you called Hal?" "No."

"Are you called Rumpelstiltskin?"

"A witch has told you! a witch has told you!" shrieked the little Man, and stamped his right foot so hard in the ground with rage that he could not draw it out again. Then he took hold of his left leg with both his hands, and pulled away so hard that his right came off in the struggle, and he hopped away howling terribly. And from that day to this the Queen has heard no more of her troublesome visitor.

123

# LITTLE ONE-EYE, TWO-EYES AND THREE-EYES

Once upon a time there was a Woman, who had three daughters, the eldest of whom was named One-Eye, because she had but a single eye, and that placed in the middle of her forehead; the second was called Two-Eyes, because she was like other mortals; and the third, Three-Eyes, because she had three eyes, and one of them in the centre of her forehead, like her eldest sister. But, because her second sister had nothing out of the common in her appearance, she was looked down upon by her sisters, and despised by her mother. "You are no better than common folk," they would say to her; "you do not belong to us"; and then they would push her about, give her coarse clothing, and nothing to eat but their leavings, besides numerous other insults as occasion offered.

Once it happened that Two-Eyes had to go into the forest to tend the goat; and she went very hungry, because her sisters had given her very little to eat that morning. She sat down upon a hillock, and cried so much that her tears flowed almost like rivers out of her eyes! By and by she looked up and saw a Woman standing by, who asked, "Why are you weeping, Two-Eyes?" "Because I have two eyes like ordinary people," replied the maiden, "and therefore my mother and sisters dislike me, push me into corners, throw me their old clothes, and give me nothing to eat but what they leave. To-day they have given me so little that I am still hungry." "Dry your eyes, then, now," said the wise Woman; "I will tell you something which shall prevent you from being hungry again. You must say to your goat:

> "*Little kid, milk*
> Table, appear!'

"and immediately a nicely filled table will stand before you, with delicate food upon it, of which you can eat as much as you please. And when you are satisfied, and have done with the table, you must say:

> "*Little kid, milk*
> Table, depart!'

"and it will disappear directly."

With these words the wise Woman went away, and little Two-Eyes thought to herself she would try at once if what the Woman said were true, for she felt very hungry indeed.

*"Little kid, milk*
Table, appear!"

said the maiden, and immediately a table covered with a white cloth stood before her, with a knife and fork, and silver spoon; and the most delicate dishes were ranged in order upon it, and everything as warm as if they had been just taken away from the fire. Two-Eyes said a short grace, and then began to eat; and when she had finished she pronounced the words which the wise Woman had told her:

*"Little kid, milk*
Table, depart!"

and directly the table and all that was on it quickly disappeared. "This is capital housekeeping," said the maiden, in high glee; and at evening she went home with her goat, and found an earthen dish which her sisters had left her filled with their leavings. She did not touch it; and the next morning she went off again without taking the meagre breakfast which was left out for her. The first and second time she did this the sisters thought nothing of it; but when she did the same the third morning their attention was roused, and they said, "All is not right with Two-Eyes, for she has left her meals twice, and has touched nothing of what was left for her; she must have found some other way of living." So they determined that One-Eye should go with the maiden when she drove the goat to the meadow and pay attention to what passed, and observe whether any one brought her to eat or to drink.

When Two-Eyes, therefore, was about to set off, One-Eye told her she was going with her to see whether she took proper care of the goat and fed her sufficiently. Two-Eyes, however, divined her sister's object, and drove the goat where the grass was finest, and then said, "Come, One-Eye, let us sit down, and I will sing to you." So One-Eye sat down, for she was quite tired with her unusual walk and the heat of the sun.

> *"Are you awake or asleep, One-Eye?*
> Are you awake or asleep?"

sang Two-Eyes, until her sister really went to sleep. As soon as she was quite sound, the maiden had her table out, and ate and drank all she needed; and by the time One-Eye woke again the table had disappeared, and the maiden said to her sister, "Come, we will go home now; while you have been sleeping the goat might have run about all over the world." So they went home, and after Two-Eyes had left her meal untouched, the mother inquired of One-Eye what she had seen, and she was obliged to confess that she had been asleep.

The following morning the mother told Three-Eyes that she must go out and watch Two-Eyes, and see who brought her food, for it was certain that some one must. So Three-Eyes told her sister that she was going to accompany her that morning to see if she took care of the goat and fed her well; but Two-Eyes saw through her design, and drove the goat again to the best feeding-place. Then she asked her sister to sit down and she would sing to her, and Three-Eyes did so, for she was very tired with her long walk in the heat of the sun. Then Two-Eyes began to sing as before:

> *"Are you awake, Three-Eyes?"*

but, instead of continuing as she should have done,

> *"Are you asleep, Three-Eyes?"*

she said by mistake,

> *"Are you asleep, Two-Eyes?"*

and so went on singing:

> *"Are you awake, Three-Eyes?"*
> *"Are you asleep, Two-Eyes?"*

By and by Three-Eyes closed two of her eyes, and went to sleep with them; but the third eye, which was not spoken to, kept open. Three-Eyes, however, cunningly shut it too, and feigned to be asleep, while she was really watching; and soon Two-Eyes, thinking all safe, repeated the words:

> *"Little kid, milk*
> Table, appear!"

127

and as soon as she was satisfied she said the old words:

> *"Little kid, milk*
> Table, depart!"

Three-Eyes watched all these proceedings; and presently Two-Eyes came and awoke her, saying, "Ah, sister! you are a good watcher, but come, let us go home now." When they reached home Two-Eyes again ate nothing; and her sister told her mother she knew now why the haughty hussy would not eat their victuals. "When she is out in the meadow," said her sister, "she says:

> *"'Little kid, milk*
> Table, appear!'

"and, directly, a table comes up laid out with meat and wine, and everything of the best, much better than we have; and as soon as she has had enough she says:

> *"'Little kid, milk*
> Table, depart!'

"and all goes away directly, as I clearly saw. Certainly she did put to sleep two of my eyes, but the one in the middle of my forehead luckily kept awake!"

"Will you have better things than we?" cried the envious mother; "then you shall lose the chance"; and so saying, she took a carving-knife and killed the goat dead.

As soon as Two-Eyes saw this she went out, very sorrowful, to the old spot and sat down where she had sat before to weep bitterly. All at once the wise Woman stood in front of her again, and asked why she was crying. "Must I not cry," replied she, "when the goat which used to furnish me every day with a dinner, according to your promise, has been killed by my mother, and I am again suffering hunger and thirst?" "Two-Eyes," said the wise Woman, "I will give you a piece of advice. Beg your sisters to give you the entrails of the goat, and bury them in the earth before the house door, and your fortune will be made." So saying, she disappeared, and Two-Eyes went home, and said to her sisters, "Dear sisters, do give me some part of the slain kid; I desire nothing else—let me have the entrails." The sisters laughed and readily gave them to her; and she buried them secretly before the threshold of the door, as the wise Woman had bidden her.

The following morning they found in front of the house a wonderfully beautiful tree, with leaves of silver and fruits of gold hanging from the boughs, than which nothing more splendid could be seen in the world. The two elder sisters were quite ignorant how the tree came where it stood; but Two-Eyes perceived that it was produced by the goat's entrails, for it stood on the exact spot where she had buried them. As soon as the mother saw it she told One-Eye to break off some of the fruit. One-Eye went up to the tree, and pulled a bough toward her, to pluck off the fruit; but the bough flew back again directly out of her hands;

and so it did every time she took hold of it, till she was forced to give up, for she could not obtain a single golden apple in spite of all her endeavors. Then the mother said to Three-Eyes, "Do you climb up, for you can see better with your three eyes than your sister with her one." Three-Eyes, however, was not more fortunate than her sister, for the golden apples flew back as soon as she touched them. At last the mother got so impatient that she climbed the tree herself; but she met with no more success than either of her daughters, and grasped the air only when she thought she had the fruit. Two-Eyes now thought she would try, and said to her sisters, "Let me get up, perhaps I may be successful." "Oh, you are very likely indeed," said they, "with your two eyes: you will see well, no doubt!" So Two-Eyes climbed the tree, and directly she touched the boughs the golden apples fell into her hands, so that she plucked them as fast as she could, and filled her apron before she went down. Her mother took them of her, but returned her no thanks; and the two sisters, instead of treating Two-Eyes better than they had done, were only the more envious of her, because she alone could gather the fruit—in fact, they treated her worse.

One morning, not long after the springing up of the apple-tree, the three sisters were all standing together beneath it, when in the distance a young Knight was seen riding toward them. "Make haste, Two-Eyes!" exclaimed the two elder sisters; "make haste, and creep out of our way, that we may not be ashamed of you"; and so saying, they put over her in great haste an empty cask which stood near, and which covered the golden apples as well, which she had just been plucking. Soon the Knight came up to the tree, and the sisters saw he was a very handsome man, for he stopped to admire the fine silver leaves and golden fruit, and presently asked to whom the tree belonged, for he should like to have a branch off it. One-Eye and Three-Eyes replied that the tree belonged to them; and they tried to pluck a branch off for the Knight. They had their trouble for nothing, however, for the boughs and fruit flew back as soon as they touched them. "This is very wonderful." cried the Knight, "that this tree should belong to you, and yet you cannot pluck the fruit!" The sisters, however, maintained that it was theirs; but while they spoke Two-Eyes rolled a golden apple from underneath the cask, so that it travelled to the feet of the Knight, for she was angry, because her sisters had not spoken the truth. When he saw the apple he was astonished, and asked where it came from; and One-Eye and Three-Eyes said they had another sister, but they dared not let her be seen, because she had only two eyes, like common folk! The Knight, however, would see her, and called, "Two-Eyes, come here!" and soon she made her appearance from under the cask. The Knight was bewildered at her great beauty, and said, "You, Two-Eyes, can surely break off a bough of this tree for me?" "Yes," she replied, "that I will, for it is my property"; and climbing up, she easily broke off a branch with silver leaves and golden fruit, which she handed to the Knight. "What can I give you in return, Two-Eyes?" asked the Knight. "Alas! if you will take me with you I shall be happy, for now I suffer hunger and thirst, and am in trouble and grief from early morning to late evening; take me, and save me!" Thereupon the Knight raised Two-Eyes upon his saddle, and took her home to his father's castle. There he gave her beautiful clothes, and all she wished for to eat or to drink; and afterward, because his love for her had become so great, he married her, and a very happy wedding they had.

Her two sisters, meanwhile, were very jealous when Two-Eyes was carried off by the Knight; but they consoled themselves by saying, "The wonderful tree remains still for us; and even if we cannot get at the fruit, everybody that passes will stop to look at it, and then come and praise it to us. Who knows where our wheat may bloom?" The morning after this speech, however, the tree disappeared, and with it all their hopes; but when Two-Eyes that same day looked out of her chamber window, behold, the tree stood before it, and there remained!

For a long time after this occurrence Two-Eyes lived in the enjoyment of the greatest happiness; and one morning two poor women came to the palace and begged an alms. Two-Eyes, after looking narrowly at their faces, recognized her two sisters, One-Eye and Three-Eyes, who had come to such great poverty that they were forced to wander about, begging their bread from day to day. Two-Eyes, however, bade them welcome, invited them in, and took care of them, till they both repented of their evil which they had done to their sister in the days of their childhood.

**THE END**

Made in the USA
Lexington, KY
03 October 2012